Gemma Roman

The Years of Us

Cover image courtesy of Rebekah Hill and Jacob Prytherch.

ISBN-13: 978-1533642899
ISBN-10: 1533642893

For news and updates, follow me on Facebook:
https://www.facebook.com/GemmaRomanBooks

Gemma Roman books

For my mum, whose inspiration led me to believe I could one day write this book . . . and who fed me wine and listened to my character's woes whenever I doubted it

Prologue:

I can't believe what I've just seen, and feel sick as I get into my car and pull out onto the street.

The amount of one way streets don't help, and I force myself to concentrate on the road as I speed towards home, knowing I need to leave my past behind and make my future count.

I had plugged in the sat nav, but it always takes a few minutes to kick in and realise where it is. Luckily I remember most of the journey so I plough on, hoping that the roads will disappear behind me like the life I could have had.

I turn the stereo up, switching radio stations until I hear some generic dance music to grab my attention with its repetitive beat. I open the window, letting in some air to keep me alert and prepare me for the motorway journey.

I change lanes, getting lost in a world of my own delayed heartbreak, as I see a headlight suddenly dart across my path. I try to swerve and push my horn, but it's too late, I hear screaming metal and a mechanical orchestra of horns.

Then nothing but darkness.

2005:

Luke

I watch her sleeping, this woman who has shared my flat and my bed for the last four years. She is beautiful. My eyes move from the curve of her cheek to the flowing line of her shoulder, with the small but intricate star tattoo visible at the back of her neck. Silky strands of hair the colour of dark chocolate meander around the inked pattern and fan out as they trail further down her back and mix with the bedclothes.

It's only 2am, but I can't sleep, so I leave Ruby to her dreams and walk through to the lounge, the clock ticking a tedious beat that seems to match that coming from my ribcage.

I'm never sure how long we've been together when someone asks. Those early University days are a slight blur, but I remember the excitement of knowing that this girl was becoming more than just my housemate. It was quite early on from what she tells me, and of course I remember the majority of it, just not specific dates.

There was one night when we watched a Guns & Roses tribute band at the local bar, and I remember her letting me stand so close behind her that I could smell her hair. It was the most intoxicating scent – something fruity and spicy – and I'm not sure what happened but it was one of the best gigs I've ever been to.

It was tough at times, living together, especially at the start. We have always had a passionate relationship, which meant that we would argue a lot: not great when you live with four other people, but things have been better since we've had our own space. I've always preferred it when it's just the two of us. There are still arguments, as with any couple, but now there are fewer bystanders.

Of course, we live close enough to our old house mates that we often congregate at one flat – Alex moved in with his girlfriend, Kate, when we got our flat – she had been in Manchester for a year studying teaching but managed to transfer after the long distance proved too much for her and their four-year relationship. They live in Southampton now, only a short train ride from us in Winchester, and he is often here with Ruby after a post work drink (they both got jobs in the local record shop after graduating from their Film Studies degrees) or sleeping on the sofa when a train journey after a night out seems too far to travel alone.

I don't mind, of course. I've known Alex for as long as Ruby and we're like brothers. We see Sam and Millie almost as often – Sam moved home for the summer after graduation, but Bradford had lost its lustre and so she was soon back here, lucky that Millie had bought a two-bedroom flat in the town centre after being left an inheritance from her grandmother and was yet to find a roommate.

With our flats within ten minutes of each other, there is rarely an evening when Ruby and I can relax alone. She doesn't mind, of course, always keen to have company or pop out for a drink. Ruby has always liked being around people, which is part of what I love about her. She has this optimistic view of the world, and she seems to exude an excitement for pretty much everything. I'm guessing this is something that will change as we get older, but for now it's amazing to be around. On the occasions when I get her to myself for a while, it's intoxicating and reminds me why I fell for her to begin with.

I'm not sure how long I've sat in the dark, but my eyes have begun to feel heavy. I pull a blanket from the back of the sofa, too sleepy to walk back through and risk waking Ruby. I curl up and succumb to a resistant slumber, only briefly wondering what Ruby will think when she finds me asleep on the sofa once again.

Kate

I have no idea how long I have been staring at the ceiling, but I know that I can't sleep because once again, my boyfriend hasn't come home. I check the bedside clock – 2.37am – and force myself to take a deep breath and shut my eyes.

I know there is no cause for alarm: he won't have been hurt. But this is the second night this week that he has been out after work and 'forgotten' to let me know he'll be late. I know that I can trust him, and that it shouldn't bother me, but I can't help wondering what he does into the small hours. Maybe if there was a group of them that ended up at the pub it wouldn't be so bad, and he says that sometimes they do start out as a group. It just happens that he and Ruby have known each other for years and happen to work together now, and need to relax after a hard day working in a record shop. Maybe if we had found a flat in Winchester, I would get invited for a drink, but Alex doesn't like to think of me getting the train to meet them in the dark. He much prefers to think of me all alone at home while he drinks with an old friend who, honestly, is probably more his type than I am.

I know he loves me, but there is something concerning about his tone when he mentions a post work trip to the pub. It's a small change, but it's noticeable. There's laughter in his voice, an excitement that he no longer has when we talk about day to day things. He has known Ruby for four years, which isn't as long as the seven years we've been together, but there's just something that makes me a little bit uneasy about their friendship. I don't know what it is, but when you spend so much time with a friend, work and leisure, you must confide a lot about your home life.

I've always had more female friends than male, and I'm happy that way. I wouldn't be friends with a man that I was attracted to, out of respect for Alex, and I would rather be at home with my boyfriend, relaxing with a film or planning for our future instead of out in some dingy pub until late at night. I know I may be in the minority there, but I'm almost twenty-four and I spend more time thinking about starting a family and buying a house than I do thinking about bands, drinking and whatever else keeps them busy until 3am. Sometimes he doesn't come home – too busy talking to get to the station for the last train. Luckily for him, there is a spare bedroom in the flat that Ruby shares with her boyfriend Luke. Though I'm not sure how happy I'd be if I was Luke and my girlfriend regularly rolled in drunk with an extra room mate.

Maybe I'm overreacting. Like I said, I trust

Alex and I don't usually lie awake worrying about him. But I'd just be interested to find out what they talk about for so long when no one else is there. The frustrating thing is that I will probably never know.

I wonder sometimes whether his friends are more important to him than I am. I know how much he loves them, and they've all chosen to stay around each other after graduating rather than disbanding like most people do. Most of my friends from University have moved back home, but with Alex so keen to stay close the best I could do was insist on living here, hoping that a train journey would coax him into spending more time with me than on drunken nights out. Unfortunately, this seems to have backfired and I am finding myself increasingly alone in a flat while he pretends to still be a student.

I have friends who met their partners at University and are now engaged, living near to their families and planning to settle and start a family. Mentioning this to Alex, however, often results in another night alone while he tells me that we should enjoy our youth and spend time with friends – there's plenty of time in the future to settle down, but we'll only have one shot at our twenties. I had thought that three years of drinking and wiling away the hours in dirty, noisy pubs was enough, but it seems I am, again, alone in my opinion there.

Ruby

My eyes open to the pleasant sound of guitars, distant and tuneful, lulling me out of my dreams. I roll over, tugging on the duvet and reach for my phone on the bed side table, to silence the alarm. 10.30 – I feel my body wishing for more of a lie in, and as I attempt to pull myself up to sit on the edge of the bed, I look to the other side . . . no Luke.

He's worked 9-5 since we graduated, but I can never get used to waking up alone. He must feel similar about going to sleep alone, but I guess that's what happens when you have different body clocks from shifts.

My phone plays me the sounds of guitars again, and I glance at the display as I turn the alarm off.

Are you awake yet? Seemed mean to wake you, I'm making coffee x

I'd forgotten Alex had stayed, but it has become a regular occurrence – our sofa is much closer than the train station when it gets late and there is another round to buy and friends to chat to. I pull on my dressing gown over my shorts and blue vest and wander into the lounge.

Alex is stood in the kitchen, wearing last night's jeans but smelling of shower gel as I lean past him to pull the bread out of the bread bin.

"Has Kate shouted at you yet for sleeping here again?" I ask playfully, adding a gesture to ask how many slices of toast he wants.

"She sent me a text late last night, I think she might have stayed up again" He gives me a guilty smile, taking three slices of bread from me and playfully pushing me into the lounge.

I wonder how their relationship works: Can you really trust your partner if they rarely come home? My friends often come to me for relationship advice, and I rarely give opinions unless requested, but I have to wonder whether he's happy with her if he only goes home every few days.

"Do you not miss going home to her when you stay here?" I ask innocently, not wanting to pry.

"Yeah, course. I've asked her before to get the train after work and come to the pub, but she's so tired after dealing with kids all day and always has lesson plans to do. She's quite a homely person, always talking about buying a house. I'm just not ready for a mortgage yet," Alex gives me a sheepish look, as if he hadn't meant to say that much.

"Kate's always seemed so settled with you, and I don't think that's bad, you've been together so long – six years now?" I ask, moving across on the sofa, as he comes to join me with hot coffee and a huge plate of melting toast.

"Almost seven, and I can't imagine being without her. I'm just not sure that we want the same things at the moment. Maybe it's because she's moved away from her family and friends to live here, and I still have all of you on my doorstep, but it just feels like we're drifting apart. I don't know," We munch quietly on the toast, watching the credits to 'This Morning' rolling across the TV screen.

I'm loathed to comment. Having been with Luke for four years, and living together for the whole time, I feel that our relationship has been more committed from the start, and yet I can't imagine being with someone for seven years. Other than Alex, most of our friends are single, so to see him choosing to spend nights here rather than with Kate makes me concerned for him. He catches my eye, sensing that I have more to say.

"What?" he asks simply, clearly wanting me to shed some hope into the conversation.

"Nothing', I begin, 'Seven years is a long time, especially at our age. It feels like we're just starting to work out who we want to be, and I can't see myself being with the same person now that I was with at 16 . . .' Alex raises an eyebrow, his lips curving into a curious smile.

"His name was Mark, he was 17 and he gave me flowers that he'd ripped up from our garden . . .

Needless to say my mum wasn't happy and the relationship didn't last long!' I snort at the memory, putting down my hot mug before it spills onto the sofa.

"That's not a good example, but I bet it makes Kate look pretty good?'

"She's amazing, and I don't want it to seem like I doubt that. Hell, looking back it doesn't even seem that anything has changed. All of our friends at home kept saying that we'd never stay together, but somehow it's worked. Everyone has ups and downs but we've always worked through our problems, and I'm still happy with her," he looks into his mug, as though searching for the right words, "I just don't know if I'm still making her happy, does that sound stupid?" his eyes find mine, looking for understanding.

"It doesn't sound stupid, but it doesn't sound like something I should answer," I tell him, unsure what he wants to hear, "Have you said any of this to Kate?"

"Not in so many words. It feels like we hardly see each other recently. She works so hard and has weekends at home, but I'm usually here and she never wants to join us all. Maybe it's my fault, maybe I should go home more and spend time with her, but with everyone here I feel like I'm missing out if I don't stay until closing time" he looks tired, and not just from our late night. I suddenly feel guilty for the nights when I'd mocked him for leaving the pub to find the train station.

"Have you thought about moving here rather than Southampton? That way you could do both, and Kate could be part of it more" I suggested, trying to ease my guilt by helping.

"I wanted to live here when we moved, and I even found places for us to look at but Kate preferred Southampton. For her, there are no ties here and she's become comfortable with her work and lifestyle there. Honestly, when we graduated, I think she wanted me to find a job nearer home and she didn't understand why I chose to work here. But to me, Southampton is just somewhere I go to try and keep her happy. I don't know," he suddenly shakes his head, as if trying to shake the thoughts away.

"Sorry, I obviously need to keep myself busy today to stop thinking through all this shit" The plate is empty, and Alex stands up abruptly to head back into the kitchen. His eyes have clouded over, so I think quickly to suggest a distraction that he obviously needs.

"Hey, it's pay day today, yeah? Why don't we go into town early and we can indulge in some retail therapy before work?"

"Sounds very girly," he winks as he makes his way back to the lounge, "but if you need to tell yourself it was for my benefit, so be it."

Millie

Someone somewhere is murdering a cat and playing loud drums.

When my pillow won't stop the noise, I look around for the culprit. My phone sits on my bedside table, lit up and vibrating as if it's proud to be depriving me of sleep.

I press the red button on my old, battered Nokia that really needs to be updated now I have a new business to run and roll over to enjoy the extra ten-minute snooze.

"Millie", there's a gentle knock on my door. I answer with a noise that I hope sounds like a snore. This obviously doesn't have the desired effect, as Sam pops her head around the door and sees my eyelids flicker.

"Millie, it's after 10. What time's your meeting?"

Oh shit.

"My meeting's at 11!" I reach for my phone again, which reads 10.09.

"Ok, there's plenty of time. Have a quick shower and I can drive you into town if you like. I've got a few bits to get, and then I'll meet you afterwards for a coffee. Sound good?" She walks over to the bedside table to set down a steaming mug of tea.

"That sounds great! Thanks Sam, I'll be ready

in 20" I stand up and stumble across to the bathroom, wishing that Ruby hadn't convinced me to have the extra pint last night.

By half past ten, I'm stood in my (only) suit – a pretty but smart black trouser suit, with a pink blouse that highlights the embroidery on the lapel of my jacket – in front of a full length mirror in the hallway. I've already attempted to tease my rebellious blonde curls into a more tamed ponytail, but they refused to oblige and instead I've given up, letting them roam free as they tumble past my shoulders. I've borrowed a pair of Sam's black patent kitten heeled shoes to add a bit of height to my five foot four frame. I add a touch of shiny, clear lip-gloss to complete the look and appraise my reflection critically.

"Nervous?" Sam asks, as she appears in her doorway, behind me.

"Yes, very" I'm trying not to think about it. The meeting is at a local bank to try and secure a small business loan. My Nan passed away last year from a sudden heart attack and we'd been really close – she left me a lot of money, which I had no idea about. She'd only been 73, and I really wasn't ready for her to leave me, but she'd always been encouraging of my dream to one day own a craft shop – she'd always come along to craft fairs I'd done, and had left me enough of her savings to buy my lovely, quaint flat and then use the rest for business start-up costs. Thankfully, that meant I had no mortgage payments to worry about, but I was a few grand short of the price of the little shop unit I'd seen for sale on the high street. Hence my meeting and I didn't want to let my lovely grandmother down, so I needed to make a good impression.

"You look fab, Millie. Your Nan would be proud" Sam gives me a quick squeeze, and glances at her watch,

"Come on, we've got twenty minutes to get you there" she grabs her keys from the bowl on the hallway table, and I take a few painkillers to numb the headache that last night has brought on.

Alex

I know she is only trying to help, but I'm not sure that a morning alone with Ruby on a spring day is helping. I love Kate, and I have no intention of doing anything disloyal, but spending so much time with a close friend who happens to be very pretty and share a lot of your interests and views is perhaps not what you should do when you're struggling to decide a future for your own relationship. I have known Ruby for years, even lived with her for a few of them, and never felt anything other than friendship for her. There's just something about being in close proximity to someone that you know so well, who you spend around eight hours a day with, that makes it tough sometimes to find the friendship line and not cross it.

The truth of the matter is, sometimes I'm so easily swayed not to go home because it's always the same – I get back and Kate will be tired from working and so will snap at me and then we'll watch TV for a few hours before she falls asleep. Honestly, I can't remember the last time we had sex, and I miss that. I guess after seven years it's expected to some extent, but I thought it was something that happened when people got older, not in their early twenties.

Ruby and I sometimes talk about this after a

few drinks, and we share similar frustrations. Maybe it's down to being on different body clocks, Ruby and me always working shifts while Kate and Luke have more of a routine, leaving them tired. Whatever it is, it's not helping to know that Ruby isn't getting the attention she wants or deserves either. I try to put the thoughts out of my head as Ruby playfully shoves me off the pavement.

"Hey, this is supposed to be cheering you up dude, it freaks me out when you give me the silent treatment!" she sticks out her tongue so far that I see the stud that cuts through it, "we have a whole town full of shops ahead of us, where would you like to spend your hard earned cash?" she makes a sweeping motion with her hand to highlight the high street in front as we plod down the hill.

"Think we should buy something new for the pub at the weekend, you keep moaning that you need new clothes, and to be fair you look a bit scruffy!" I mock, giving her a quick wink and shoving her across the pavement, giving me room to regain my walking space at her side.

"Ha! Says the guy with holes in his jeans" I realise this is true.

"I bought them like this, its called fashion!" I point out, to which I receive a small sneer as we reach a little clothes boutique on the corner.

I turn to ask Ruby if she wants to try inside,

but she's already ambling through the door. She walks past the sales assistant with a confident smile and begins rummaging through the racks.

"Whoa, Alex, you should try this on, green looks good on you" She hands me a shirt with a psychedelic purple and green print. I take it, the pattern almost putting me into a trance as she strides over to a floaty short dress, black with silver spots covering it. She finds her size before her eyes light up, spotting something else at the back of the shop. I've been shopping with her before, something we often do before or after work – and though she has a hippy, quirky style of her own, she loves shopping and she tends to have a knack for finding 'hidden treasures' as she calls them in little shops such as this.

I browse around, finding another shirt, some jeans and a long sleeved top to try on and find Ruby looking at shoes as I emerge from the fitting room with jeans and the shirt Ruby found tucked under my arm.

"Ready?" I ask her, and she looks at me sheepishly, glancing at the stool next to her. She's added a few more items since I left her with a dress in hand, so I raise my eyebrows and she removes the high heels adorned with multi-coloured skulls and puts her converse back on. We pay for our things and leave the shop, feeling slightly better for some retail therapy, I must admit.

We often joke that Ruby and I got half of each other's personality – while I am a red blooded male with no doubt of my orientation, I enjoy wine and shopping and tend to over analyse. Ruby would rather be in male company, has a keen interest in horror films and often points out attractive women to our single friends in the pub. These traits are probably partly why we have such a strong friendship and enjoy each other's company, but sometimes cause me to analyse my own relationship too much. Kate doesn't really have any male friends, which may be why she struggles to understand my friendship with Ruby. Regardless of today's mood, I have never been unfaithful or given Kate any reason to doubt my fidelity. My phone beeps in my pocket and I retrieve it to look at the display.

Hey babe, did you get my text? I hate when you don't come home. Let me know you're ok, miss you. K xx

I realise guiltily that I haven't replied to last night's text. The shop comes into view, so I type a quick reply promising to be home later, and put my phone away as Ruby glances at me with raised eyebrows.

"Is everything OK?" she smiles, hopeful that my mood hasn't dropped into brooding territory again.

"Fine, think we have time to buy a few CDs before work?" I return her smile, beginning to chuckle as I watch her eyes glint mischievously. We pick up the pace, heading for the sale racks to try and grab a few bargains in the fifteen minutes before we start our shifts.

Sam

I put on my simple fuchsia pumps and look in the mirror: The shoes are a favourite for work, remaining comfy for a full shift, but the colour giving my outfit an extra lift.

Getting ready for a shift at the Night Light is always interesting – there is no dress code as such, so I'm able to let my personality out to play through my clothes. It's a quirky, fun bar that opened a few months after we graduated and made us glad we'd stayed on (or in my case, moved back) It has floor to ceiling windows at the front, with a green door in the middle. The floors are all wooden and shiny, and dotted with black tables and corner booths.

I'd done a lot of bar work while studying for my Drama degree, and always enjoyed the atmosphere and tips. Luckily, a friend from my course had worked at the Night Light and recommended me for a job when we'd gone for a drink upon my return. I work most nights, but Millie often hangs out there with whoever is free and likes to control the vintage style jukebox or watch any local bands that we can get to play.

Today, I've opted for a fairly casual look of skinny jeans and a black backless top that ties at the small of my back with a pink bow, matching my shoes nicely. I add my lip gloss and phone to my bag and apply some wax to the crop of jet black (this month) mess that is my hair, walking through to the lounge, where Millie is flicking through TV channels.

"If you're still waiting for the bank to get back to you, then you might as well come for a few drinks. It's not as if we have a house phone" I say calmly.

"True, Ruby already asked if you were working. Apparently, Alex has to go back home tonight, but Luke is meeting her from work so they can meet us there" Millie reaches for her phone to confirm the evening's plans.

"Cool, it's a shame about Alex though. When was the last time that Kate joined us? It'll be funny to see Luke, alone with all the ladies!" We giggle at the thought: Luke always plays the part of the Alpha male in a large group, but whenever we'd seen him on his own, he'd become shy and quiet.

"Come on then, I need a drink!" Millie says, having changed out of her suit as soon as we'd got home, only now needing to grab her bag and coat.

Kate

I hear Alex's key in the lock, and my eyes dart to the bedside clock from my magazine – 8.42pm. To his credit, he must have rushed home to be back by now. I call through so he knows where I am, and I get up to welcome him home.

"Hey baby" I say, nuzzling his neck as soon as he walks into the bedroom. He kisses me lightly on the cheek, walking past me to remove his coat.

"How was your day?" He asks, looking tired and taking his phone from his pocket.

"Busy! Last few weeks before half term are crap!" I reply, hoping he's not as grumpy as he seems. "How was yours?"

"Crap, to be honest. Some idiot came in for a refund on a game that his kids had bought and he went crazy at Ruby for refusing him. Security had to intervene in the end, and she got a bit upset when he'd left" His anger is apparent, and I move closer to try and hug him.

"Sorry, I'm all hot and sweaty from the journey. I need a shower" he pulls away and walks past me, though it feels as if he's walked through me.

"Can't it wait until the morning? I'll be heading to bed in an hour or so" I ask gently; this isn't the evening I'd envisioned.

"Babe, I've had a shit day and I've rushed

back to see you. I'll be ten minutes, what more do you want?" He looks at me then, channelling the day's emotion into a single pointed gaze. It silences me into submission.

"I'll be in the lounge" I say quietly, handing him a towel and wondering why he lets working in a shop affect him so much.

He closes the bathroom door, and then starts the shower. After a few seconds, I hear a buzzing and realize he's left his phone on the bed.

I walk over to it, knowing I should respect his privacy but curiosity wins out and I pick it up.

Glad you got home safe, missing my drinking buddy though. Thanks for cuddles after today – you smelt nice too! ;) See you in the morning x

I don't even have to look at the name, but somehow feel winded by the intimacy of the message. I throw the phone back on the bed as if its' burnt me, and walk through to the lounge pretending that I don't feel the prickle of tears behind my eyelids.

Ruby

I sit down on the bed and gently caress Luke's shoulder. Sadly, weekends are usually early starts for me and they are the only lazy mornings that Luke has. I do miss the lazy student days when we were first together; full of sex, bacon sandwiches and hangover reducing coffee. Luke turns over without waking, and settles into a steady snore. His hand lands on his head, absently touching the spot near his ear where his straw-coloured hair has started to creep down. He's always liked it short, but I have to admit I quite like when it looks a bit more rugged.

Every so often, he'll get caught up with a busy week at work and let his stubble grow for a while, until he can't bear the tickle against his chin. This has been one of those weeks, and I relish the chance to watch how the extra hair softens his face, knowing that he'll probably have shaved by the time I'm home from work. I can't resist reaching out and touching my fingertips to the bristle at his jaw line, smiling mischievously as his muscular arm moves from under the covers to scratch the itch I've created.

There's a quiet knock at the door, so I kiss Luke on the forehead and have a last glance around for anything I've forgotten to put in my bag.

Out in the lounge, I open the door to a very sleepy looking Alex.

"Good morning sleepy face" I say with a smile, as I lock the door behind me.

"Don't start you" he says, with a smile in his voice that doesn't reach his eyes.

"You ok?" I ask, giving him a smile that he can't seem to reciprocate.

"Yeah, don't ask" he says with a sigh, refusing to meet my eye.

"At least you're not hung over?" I try, and from the curve of his lip I see my tactic worked. At that point, both of our phones bleep.

I got the loan!! Celebratory drinks tonight – Sam's working. Night light at 8? Don't make me drink alone – I'm a business woman now! x

"Sounds like a plan, and you seem like you need to drown some sorrows?" I glance up at Alex, who seems to be coming out of his mood.

"I think so, sorry. Just didn't sleep well. Kate was really off with me after I'd rushed back to see her. I'll let her know I'll be late tonight, we can't miss Millie's big celebration" He replies, his smile back where it belongs. We walk slowly towards the shop, Alex lost in his thoughts and me myself, relieved that I've bought a new dress for the evening.

Alex

I lay awake for hours last night, wondering what had happened to the relationship that had meant everything to me a year ago. It wasn't the relationship that I'd grown sick of; it was the fact that I wasn't sure what we had in common anymore. I felt like I needed time to see if it was what I really wanted, rather than something I'd got trapped into. I'd watched the patch in the ceiling where the paint was peeling away, until I got so restless I had to get up and watch films. I'd been in the middle of Tenacious D – Pick of Destiny when the alarm had told me I needed to get ready for work.

I now stand in front of a customer, who can't understand our ordering process, zoning out slightly until Ruby catches my eye and walks over.

"Everything alright over here?" she asks the elderly gentleman, who mutters something about asking his wife's permission before stumbling out of the door.

"You look awful, good job we finish in ten minutes" Ruby winks at me, moving to help a customer so I can escape the shop floor for a few minutes.

I check my phone in the staff room and see the voice mail icon, so I take it into the toilets with me. I hold the phone to my ear and listen.

"Hi babe, I'm sorry if I was quiet last night. I've not been feeling well and got a bit worried. I did a test this morning; please ring me back when you get this. I love you"

After seven years together, this isn't the first scare we've had, but it's the first time I've been told over the phone, and the first time I feel sick at the prospect. I run the cold tap and throw the water on my face. Looking at myself in the mirror, I'm ashen and feel like I can't breathe. I have to get home, now. I open the door and see Ruby in front of me.

"Sorry, I have to get home" I mutter in a blur, brushing past her and almost forgetting to pick up my coat on the way out.

Kate

I know I shouldn't have left that message, but after seeing the text last night I panicked. I can't lose Alex, not after the years that we've put into this relationship. I needed to do something that would make him realise how good we are together; the future we have. I'd phoned Alex and then opened the bottle of wine in the fridge. I'm on my second glass when I text my sister, Ali, for advice. Five minutes later, the phone rings.

"What the hell have you done?!" her usually bubbly voice sounds clipped.

"I know, but I panicked. I didn't see the other messages, but this text was so . . . Intimate somehow. Like – "she cuts me off

"Somehow, like they've been friends for years? Come on, Kate, you don't really think he'd go behind your back? And even so, isn't lying a bit risky?" She sounds almost angry, making me wonder why I'd asked her in the first place. I walk into the kitchen, suddenly in need of more alcohol.

"I know, I shouldn't have said I was pregnant, but I didn't know what else to do. He's never here, Ali. You don't understand. I moved here to be with him, and I'm home alone while he's out with his friends" I sink into a stool, tracing a chip in the marble counter with my finger.

"I know it must be hard there on your own,

why don't you go out and meet his friends? Trust me, I'm 30 – you'll get to my age and realise you should have enjoyed your twenties" Ali has always been the outgoing sister, but I know she means well.

"Maybe, I don't know. What do I say when he comes home? Should I tell him the truth?" I wonder aloud.

"Either that or you'll have a lot to explain in nine months. Oh hun, talk to him. You'll work it out, just ring me when you've spoken to him" Ali hangs up, and I know she's right. To be honest, I'm not sure what made me leave that message; I just couldn't get that text from Ruby out of my head. I stand up and turn back to the lounge to put the phone back. That's when I look up and see Alex staring at me.

Luke

I'm sat on the sofa, drinking beer and watching a Star Wars marathon when Ruby's face peeks round the front door.

"Hey!" she pulls me up to standing and gives me a quick hug.

"Hey babe, did you have a good day?" I smile at her, realising as I sway slightly that I'm halfway through a six-pack of beer already.

"Yeah, thanks. Alex was a bit weird at the end though. I'll have to investigate at the pub" she winks at me

"You're going out again? I'd thought maybe a pizza and the rest of Star Wars" I slump back on the sofa, deflated.

"*We've* been invited out to celebrate Millie's loan being accepted for her shop. Don't tell me you're turning down a night with friends? I'll have to buy you some slippers for your next birthday!" Her tongue stud peeks out through her lips, and I sigh.

"I never get you to myself, do I?" I stand up, hoping that we can get away with leaving early. I like nights out at the pub, but I miss nights at home with my girlfriend.

Alex

"You lied to me?!" I sit on the bed, staring at this woman who I've loved for the best part of a decade, and for the first time I see betrayal and distrust in her eyes.

She holds my gaze and I see tears filling up those beautiful eyes, though she doesn't reply. She sinks to her knees, her cropped dark hair falling around her face.

"Kate?" I whisper, reaching my hand out to brush the hair behind her ear. It feels too intimate a gesture after the day's events, but I still can't stand to see her upset.

"I'm sorry" She mumbles, a tear escaping as she tries to blink them back.

"I'm not looking for an apology; I need an explanation. Why would you do this?!" My voice rises as I look into her eyes once more.

"I thought that if there was a baby, you might spend more time at home . . . I'm here most nights alone, and that's not how I saw this happening" Kate sighs, and lets out a sob.

"You pretended you were having my baby so I'd spend time with you?! Do you hear how messed up that sounds?" I can feel myself getting angry; I can't see how someone I thought I knew and loved could deceive me like this.

"That's not how I meant it, but it's so lonely

here without you. I feel like most days I don't even cross your mind, like you'd rather you were with someone who wanted the same things you do"

"This is about me being friends with Ruby?" I lock eyes with her, not comprehending what I'm hearing.

"You don't see how it looks from the outside; you're always getting drunk and staying on her sofa. You hardly ever come home, so what am I meant to think?" I get to my feet to give myself time to answer without shouting.

"You honestly think I'd be unfaithful to you? After seven years?" I can't believe what I'm hearing, how could she not trust me?

"Alex, of course I trust you, but when you spend more nights at Ruby's flat than ours, how am I meant to feel?" Kate's eyes grow wide, questioning me.

"Ruby and Luke – her boyfriend lives there too. You can't turn this around on me and make it my fault that you lied!" I walk to the window, needing to look away and pace a little.

"I'm sorry I lied, but I'm not sorry that it's given us the first night alone together that we've had in weeks. I'm not happy Alex, and I'm not sure you've even noticed" Kate stands, and comes towards me. She reaches for my hand, but I pull it away.

"You think I've been happy? I'm trying to

enjoy life while we can, before we settle down and I thought you were with me on that, at least to start with. I thought you'd get your own friends through work and we'd have some fun for a few years before things got serious. But you don't want to go out, all you want to do is talk about houses and babies, and I don't want that, not yet" I stare at her while finally letting all of this out, seeing her tears grow until they fall onto her blotchy skin.

"We've been together for seven years, Alex. Most people are married by now; I thought that was what you wanted when we first talked about living together?"

"Name a couple our age who have been together longer than a few years?" I ask her, and she's cut short.

"You can't assume that just because we've had a long time together that we should settle down before we're both ready, and even if we were, how the fuck can you justify telling me that your pregnant, when you know it's a lie?" Kate opens her mouth to answer, but closes it again when she realises she has no defence.

"I need some time" I tell her, grabbing my jacket from the bed and heading for the door.

"Where will you go?" she asks as I walk through the lounge, but I don't reply. I don't see any point in making the situation worse by adding to the lies.

Sam

I lean across to give Ruby the change for her round when her phone lights up on the bar. She picks it up and reads the message that has come through, her face painting a picture of shock.

"What's wrong hun?" I ask, noticing a group of students on their way to order some drinks.

"Oh nothing, Sam. I just need to run out and meet someone. Tell Luke I'll be back in a few minutes, would you?" At my nod, she grabs her bag and scuttles towards the door.

I begin to serve the group, one of the guys smiling at me coyly as I place a beer bottle in front of him. He rewards me with a wink and I smile back as Luke's voice cuts into my reverie.

"Sam, did you send Ruby somewhere?" he looks a little worried, at which point I realise that Ruby's round of drinks are still on the bar.

"She just had to go and meet someone she said", I give him a smile that doesn't quite meet my eyes as the cute, winking student retreats back to his friend's table, and I see a girl kiss him on the cheek in return for the Malibu and diet coke that he passes to her. I turn back to give Luke my full attention, but he has stormed off back to talk to Millie with the drinks in his hands. I should really stop flirting with students.

Ruby

I round the corner by the train station, and before I reach the door I see the black converse and messy blonde hair that I see most days. Just now, though, they are part of a crumpled little soul sat on the bench near the station entrance. He looks up and catches my gaze, his eyes a mixture of anger and hurt.

"What happened?" I sit next to him, reaching for his hand so that it will stop its aimless search for something to hit.

"She lied, she flat out lied!" He moves as if to stand, but seems to change his mind as his fingers register mine. I give his hand a gentle squeeze.

"Lied about what?" I ask, searching his face for the rest of the story.

"Ruby, she said she was pregnant" He looks at me again, and saying the words aloud seems to have been as overwhelming to say as they are to hear. Kate wouldn't do this, surely? It must be a misunderstanding.

"She's pregnant?" I look deeper into his eyes; the fear I saw as he ran out of work now making more sense.

"No, she said she was. She fucking lied to me. How the hell can she do that?" Alex stands up and begins pacing the pavement next to the bench.

"Sorry, Alex, slow down. Start from the

beginning" I stay on the bench, watching him as he tries to rid himself of the angry energy.

"Kate left a voicemail today saying that she thought she was pregnant, but needed to talk to me. So, I rushed home to see her", he stops to turn to me and push his hair from his eyes, "I got back to the flat, and she was on the phone. She didn't see me come in, but she was arguing that lying to me was the only thing she could do" He stops pacing again, and slumps back onto the bench, defeated.

"Who was on the phone?" I ask, confused.

"I don't know, her sister maybe. She's always talking to her sister. The point is, she turned round and saw me standing there and her face just masked over. I've been with her for seven years and not once have I felt betrayed like today" I look at his face, and see that his eyes have become red rimmed, shining with hurt.

"Oh Alex" I don't know what to say, so I tuck myself into him and hold him as he tries to quell the tears that threaten to spill out.

Millie

"What happened to everyone?" I sit down on a bar stool, my hands landing too hard on the counter just to signify to anyone who wasn't aware, that I've drunk a little too much.

Sam is cleaning the counter, and expertly diverts the cloth from where my hands rest.

"Well babe, it's almost eleven, so most people have gone home. Ruby ran off and never returned – not sure what that was about – and Luke seemed to get bored a while later and skulked off" Her eyebrows rise to show her lack of faith that most of our friends deserted me on my celebratory night.

I watch as Sam's eyes scan the rest of the bar, alighting on the only remaining full table. There are a group of students that look familiar, perhaps because we've shared a bar for a few hours, or perhaps because we've met them before. I turn back to Sam just in time to see her face change from the cheeky smile that I've seen many times before.

"Which one are you flirting with?" I ask her, matching her smile with a smirk of my own.

"What? I'm not flirting!" She gives a shocked snort of laughter, and turns away to clear away used glasses.

"Hey, how come Alex never arrived?" I ask,

trying to get the last sip from my beer before Sam snatches it from my hand

"I think you've finished it", she giggles at me and I realise I've been sat here drinking for a few hours without seeing a mirror.

"I don't know about Alex. Maybe Kate made him stay at home?" I use all my energy to attempt – unsuccessfully - to jump elegantly from the stool.

"I'm going to the ladies, don't lock up without me" As I saunter off towards the back of the bar, I see one of the very cute students approach Sam, and manage a smile at her false innocence before the door closes behind me.

Alex

Ruby walks with me for an hour or so, until I have exhausted myself with talking and crying. I know I can't go home tonight; I couldn't look Kate in the face and know that anger wouldn't resurface. I need time, I need a friend. I need Ruby to renew my faith in women.

We start to get cold and so we duck into a pub that we find near the station; we have walked in a huge circle and are both in need of a warming drink.

"So, what will you do?" She asks, handing over money for the drinks. We've opted for red wine over the usual beers, needing warmth and comfort from the cold night.

"I don't know, I feel so blind sighted", I take the glasses to a cosy sofa in the corner, as acoustic music thrums through a nearby speaker. I sink into the squishy seat and sigh, surveying the little place that we've happened upon. The room is dimly lit with night lights on each table, which give a subtle ambience to the warm, almost terracotta lights dotted around overhead. The floor and tables are all wooden, and most of the seats are either sofas like ours or smaller armchairs, all in similar shades of blues and greens from aqua to emerald.

Ruby catches my eye, smiling and raising her glass as well as her eyebrows to show that she's just as impressed at the little space we've just found unassumingly.

"You just need some time, stay with us tonight and see how you feel in the morning. It's a lot to process, but I'm sure you'll work it out" Ruby settles next to me, and takes a sip of her Merlot.

"I've had enough of my problems for a night; though I will take the sofa if that'll be OK with Luke?" I ask, glancing across to her.

"Its fine, Luke doesn't mind. He'll be asleep by the time we get home – ", Ruby suddenly puts her hand to her forehead and closes her eyes.

"Shit! I left him at the Night Light. I've not checked my phone, it's been ages!" She delves into her small bag to retrieve it, making a face at the screen.

"It's been on silent. Bollocks! What time is it? Luke's left me messages, I'll just text him so he knows we're OK", I tell her that it's before 11 and she punches some buttons on her phone before settling it back into her bag.

"More wine?" I ask, realising that we've both emptied our glasses. I wander to the bar as she settles back on the sofa.

Ruby

I succumb to the feeling as we sit down on my sofa, drunk more with lust than the alcohol we've consumed. It had been so long since either of us has felt real intimacy that it intoxicates us.

He pulls me close, his lips dancing on my collarbone before his mouth finds my ear.

"Have you ever wondered what this would feel like?" he asks, as he searches my face for the lust he obviously feels. My pulse quickens and, rather than admit it, I answer by pulling him to me and kissing him. I'm used to the scent of mint shower gel mixed with his spicy aftershave, but not like this. His teeth gently bite on my lower lip, his tongue venturing past my lips to find mine. After a few seconds, I remember my surroundings, the man sleeping in my bed, and the girl waiting for Alex at home. I pull away, reaching for his hand with mine.

"We can't . . . "I whisper, looking into his eyes for a look of recognition, of agreement.

"Shhhh…" Ignoring me, he kisses my cheek, my neck, my mouth. His fingers trace the line of my jaw, before locking his eyes with mine, his pupils enlarged with lust.

"Alex, stop – "I tug my face away from him, my lips bruised from their first passionate encounter in months.

"I'm sorry…" Alex turns away, standing up and walking towards the window.

The gravity of what we've just done envelops me, and I turn away. My eyes wander to the bedroom, where I realise Luke's not sleeping as I'd thought. He is wide awake and staring at me through the hazy light.

"Get out" Luke hasn't moved, but his voice and eyes both speak clearly to Alex.

Alex, still looking out at the moonlight, flinches for a fraction of a second. He refuses to meet my eye, but walks quickly towards the door and doesn't look back.

Sam

My eyes open lazily, and alight on the hand that lies across my shoulder. I roll away enough to sit on the edge of the bed and look across at the stranger who lies beside me, sleeping peacefully.

He's still very cute, as I knew he would be – His thick dark hair all ruffled and falling into his eyes. Those eyes I remember vividly from last night, a deep green with tiny flecks of amber. I'd never seen eyes so intense, and even though he'd been drinking at the bar, those eyes never left me from the moment he took my hand after I'd locked the doors to the minute they succumbed to sleep just a few hours ago. Even with his eyes closed, he's gorgeous. His long limbs somehow gracefully splayed out, the duvet slipping down almost to his hips. I feel the colour rise into my cheeks as I stare unashamedly at his muscled torso, remembering a few highlights of our night together.

At least meeting students at work, I know I don't make drunken mistakes when deciding to take someone home. I don't do it often, but who wants the pressures of a relationship? I see all the drama that unfolds with our friends and it makes me happy enough to enjoy the sex more than the relationship part, and I've never met anyone who's changed my mind as yet.

His eyes blink awake as I move to stand. He smiles and leans across the bed, his fingers brushing my hips enough to make me sit back down.

"Hey", I mirror his smile.

"Hey gorgeous, where are you going?" He pulls me to him, placing a kiss on my shoulder.

"Just thought you might like some coffee?" I ask, losing myself for a second in his embrace.

"I'll pass on the coffee, but I'd like some more of you" He purrs, his hand moves from my waist up to caress my arm, my cheek and he moves in to kiss me.

The morning after is not usually like this, most guys tend to leave for 'early lectures' or some even leave before I wake. It does save the awkwardness, but this is new. I feel my heart start to beat faster as his hand finds my breast and starts to tease my nipple.

I close my eyes, enjoying the feeling that makes my breath shorter. Desire takes over from the tiredness, and as I let it take over, I decide I much prefer this kind of morning after.

Alex

"Go ahead, tell me that it meant nothing" I look at Ruby, watching the colour rise in her cheeks as she mentally replays the kiss that awoke us both.

"Alex, we were drunk. It was just a mistake" She moves to walk past me, out of the stock room where she'd been sent to search for a CD for one of the regular customers. I'd been in here searching for replenishments, but had abandoned my work when the sight of her made my stomach flip upside down. I step into her path.

"If it was a mistake, why did you kiss me back?" I look into her eyes for an answer that I know won't come.

"We're both with other people, it was just a moment of weakness – too many drinks" I'm stood close to her, and suddenly the mark on her cheek catches my eye.

"Too many drinks? Is that what it takes for Luke to do this?" I trace the skin around the bruise, wondering how many times he's hurt her. She flinches, as if she expects me to do the same, but she doesn't move my hand away.

"He saw us, and to be fair he had a right to be angry" Ruby takes a step back, letting her long, dark hair fall into her face to conceal the tears in her eyes.

"He had a right to be angry, but at me. He had

no right to ever touch you like that" The anger that has been building in my chest threatens to bubble to the surface.

"I never should have let you – "

"He hit you, Ruby!" I lose my temper; confused at what point in her thought process it becomes arguable that violence is acceptable.

"I love him, Alex. I can't flick a switch and turn that off. Maybe you can – "I stop her

"You think I can? You think if I could turn off feelings, I wouldn't turn off whatever's happening with us? "When I look down at her, there's a vulnerability in her eyes that makes me want to hold her. I reach for her and she doesn't pull away.

"Alex, please. Don't do this" she looks into my eyes, asking me not to show her the affection and intimacy that she wants and needs.

"So stop me" I whisper, as I pull her towards me, bringing my lips to her cheek. I feel the heat of the bruise as I kiss it, hating myself for sending Luke silent thanks for doing the only thing that would send Ruby in need of comfort, into my embrace. She lets me hold her for a few seconds, until the till bell rings and she pulls away.

"They need help out there" She mutters, brushing past me without letting herself look at me.

I try to ignore the sparks that fly just from feeling her shoulder as she walks past me, and instead think of the help that is needed in here to stop me from falling for someone who isn't mine to love.

2007: (2 Years Later)
Sam

"Wow, Millie! It looks fantastic!" I'm standing in Millie's shop. It took her a long time to get through the paperwork and legal speak but she finally got into her gorgeous little store. The company that had owned it before had left in a rush, and there was some work to be done.

"I know, thought you should see it first, after all the help you've given" She gives me a quick hug, and we share a tired glance after all the late nights painting and sanding.

Since that evening at the Night Light celebrating Millie's loan approval, Ben (my gorgeous and reliable student) and I had helped Millie to get the shop ready for the grand opening this weekend. Obviously, the structural work needed professionals, but when that was finished we had been here helping her to realise her craft shop dream.

The duck-egg blue front door opens – with its own bell that lets out a sweet little tinkly chiming sound – onto a laminate floor space that manages to be roomy and cosy at the same time. There are long tables around the magnolia walls which are covered in pretty, multi-coloured tablecloths. In the far corner is the till point (a much-needed brand new cash register ordered online a few months ago) set up on a vintage style wooden desk that Millie had found at a car boot sale, and then sanded and painted the same pale blue as the door.

A small door just behind the desk leads into the tiny office, which holds another desk (this one bought from the local furniture shop) and a framed photograph on the wall above of Millie and her nan smiling gleefully at the camera, their hands both holding ice cream cones. A little archway leads through to the 'kitchen' which basically houses a small counter top with a kettle, a microwave and a sink.

"So, are you ready for Saturday's opening?" I ask her now, looking around in wonder at all the stock that she's started to display since I saw the completed shell a week ago.

"Almost there, just have a few more tables to fill, but I'm so happy with what we've done" She looks at me, her eyes welling up in gratitude.

"Hey, don't you get sentimental. Of course we helped. It's good for Ben to get used to hard work after all those sport science lectures!" We giggle, though I'm secretly thrilled that I managed to break my one-night rule with a guy as great as Ben. He was smitten from the start, so Millie says, though I never believe her. Having said that, almost two years later he's still here and has been a great source of muscle in Millie's shop.

"Fair enough!" She laughs and moves a rack

full of skull shaped beads in different colours onto the front table.

"Anyway, we should get going. I told you Ruby was back in town and wanted to catch up tonight?" I look at Millie, catching the wary look in her eyes.

"I know; it's been ages. She's back for a while though, and I'm working. The least you can do is come for a few drinks after all the hard work that Ben and I have put in for you!" I turn back to her with a mischievous glint in my eye. She laughs, which comes out as yelp, as I run for the door.

Alex

My eyes open, but refuse to focus. Sunlight glints onto the window sill, and as I flinch away my eyes catch the display on my bedside clock. It must be broken as it reads 16:32. I roll over and somehow land on the palm of a hand that seems to be buried in a river of blonde hair.

This momentarily confuses me, until the daily wave of nausea kicks in and reminds me what my life has become. My head begins to pound as I struggle to leave my bed without waking the nameless blonde, who remains asleep and snoring on Kate's side of the bed. Thinking of Kate's name makes me increase my speed en route to the bathroom, as I begin to feel lightheaded.

After relieving my stomach, I force myself to stand and look in the mirror. The grey, dishevelled face staring back seems to laugh at me with a sad, silent irony. I remember happy days in this room, when I would shave while watching Kate sleep in the mirror. Those days are a distant memory, which I apparently choose to wash away with alcohol and one night stands. If only it were that simple.

Each time I bring someone home, I see Kate's smile on their face. I hear her laugh when I try to be charming. Usually by the time I turn the key in the door, I am way past drunk and so my imagination takes over. If I were in a clear state of mind, I would perhaps move to a flat that doesn't have her written all over it. Unfortunately, since she left on that horrible rainy May afternoon, I am ashamed to say that I have not had, nor wanted, a day full of clarity. It would make me despise myself and my actions more than I do already. Instead, I drink and hope that my boss won't notice, then sleep away the day and hope that whoever I've taken home won't notice. Not the healthiest lifestyle, but one day maybe I'll look in the mirror and not be as disgusted with who I see as I am today.

Sam

I look up from behind the bar to see Alex finally arrive for his shift, twenty minutes late.

A year ago, my boss moved away to run a pub in Devon, and head office decided that I'd paid my dues enough to be given a chance at management. Having worked my ass off for a few years, I jumped at the chance to run my own bar.

Once I'd found my feet, a familiar face came knocking at my door. Around the time that I met Ben was around the time that Alex, Ruby and Luke took a step back from the group. Millie and I had never worked out why, though it seemed that both relationships had ended abruptly and badly. We'd tried to reach out to them, and still heard from Ruby occasionally, but she'd left the music shop to go travelling and we didn't see the boys for a while after that.

One night I'd been clearing tables, after a few months of managing the Night Light alone, and Alex had knocked gently on the door. I let him in, with the bar still open for half an hour, and he collapsed into a booth as I removed dirty pint glasses from it. He'd had some 'creative differences' with the new management of the shop and needed a job. I looked at him as I wiped down the table, and saw the ghost of my old friend. He looked hurt, tired and in need of help. So, I helped him. He'd somehow lost his job, his best friend and his girlfriend within months of each other, so I offered to train him as a barman. Turned out he was more of a flirt with students than I had been.

"Sorry Sammy, the train was delayed", he says as he walks past me towards the staff room. I can smell alcohol on his breath, and I catch his eye with a warning that I hope I don't need to vocalise.

I nod to Nick, my Assistant Bar Manager, to watch the bar as I follow Alex through to the staff area.

"Are you ok?" I ask, hoping I can keep the line between friend and boss clear.

"Fine, just hate trains" He avoids my eye line as he removes his jacket and hangs it up on a peg.

"Alex, I saw you drinking after your shift last night. It seemed to get a bit messy before you left, especially with that blonde", I manage to lock eyes with him before his cloud over with regret and something else I can't quite read.

"Doesn't it always? Look, Sam I apologised for being late but surely what I do off duty is my own business? Besides, I can't count how many men I saw you with when you were a lowly barmaid" His eyes caught mine then, having regained their sharp blue edge like a beautiful wave that threatened to drown you if you trusted it. He stalked out into the main bar, leaving me speechless and wondering what had happened to the friend that I'd given a lifeline to.

Ruby

I stare at my reflection, trying to ignore the dark circles under my eyes as I cover them with concealer and marvel at how much things can change in a few years.

I have spent the last eighteen months wondering where my life will lead, now that it will obviously not take the shape that I'd expected. Things never turn out as you think, I'm learning that. I hadn't expected the loss of friendship along the way though, and that had really saddened me.

Luke left the day after he'd hit me, as neither of us could see a way past what we had both done to each other. I decided to travel and clear my head for a while, since nothing seemed to make sense anymore. I'd handed in my notice at work and spent six months travelling with a friend from my Film Studies course. Amy was impulsive, fun and exactly what I had needed to be around. We had been halfway across Australia when she had learned of a death in her family and needed to return to England. I could have stayed and continued alone, but I'd seen enough horror films with Alex to decide to accompany Amy back to Winchester and try to concentrate on my future again.

I've been back for a few months, but have been a bit wary to get back in touch with the others. Luke wasn't around, but no one else knew why I'd left so I was struggling to find work and ready to give up and move back home when I happened across the Night Light one afternoon and stumbled inside to find Sam.

My old friend was alone and bored, and more than happy to reminisce with a beer (for me) and a smile (for her). She'd said that Millie was still around, and ready to celebrate the shop opening, and all I needed was some familiar faces and a reason to lose myself in more drinks.

That was almost a week ago, and now I felt strangely nervous to catch up with the old crowd again. I've done nothing but run away from my problems, and Sam seemed to have no idea about that. I'm not surprised that Luke didn't want to share the nature of our demise from our friends, as I'm not sure I'll ever be ready to speak of it again. The only person that I'd feel comfortable enough to share it with is Alex, and that's only because he was there. The one regret that I have is not staying in touch with him, the one friend that I could ring at 2am for no reason. Maybe one day we'll reconnect, but for now I'm happy to catch up with whatever friends I find.

Alex

As I wipe down a few tables, I try to avoid Sam's eye line.

I know I'm not her favourite person, but I really need this job. The waves of nausea have subsided thanks to the water that I've been drinking at the bar, and the vodka that I've been sneaking into the staff room in shot glasses every half an hour to stop my stomach from its constant spasms.

I now look up as the door opens, and my heart stops. Looking back at me is the woman who ruined my life. Or, to clarify here, was the catalyst for me ruining my own life.

It's been nineteen months, and the fact that I've counted makes me want to take another shot glass into the staff room. My head starts to swim with all of the things that I want to say to her, but it all fades into the back of my head as she locks eyes with me and I actually see her brain kick into gear and wonder what the fuck she's going to say.

"Alex?" For opening lines, it's weak. It's quite obviously me.

"Ruby" I hate myself for wishing I'd checked my appearance before my shift.

"Sam didn't mention you were working here" I see her gaze drift to Sam, who is currently making drinks for a group dressed in suits. I have no decent reply for this, so instead I smile and wish that we could rewind the last few years to when we made sense of each other's lives.

"So, how have you been?" I ask, suddenly realising that I'm wringing the cleaning cloth between my hands.

"Good thanks, travelling mainly" I look at her properly, seeing the remains of a tan that must have lit her skin into a golden glow. I hate myself again for noticing this.

"Sounds good, did you travel alone?" I swear, if she travelled and fell in love with some bronzed, toned surfer dude, I'll drink the whole vodka bottle in one sitting.

"No actually, remember Amy from the course?" As she speaks, I feel a penny drop that falls into the sea that is my year long hangover. I remember Amy, the blonde girl that I always found attractive in that cute way that girls seem when they're so keen to experience the world. The blonde girl who disappeared, and who I thought I saw again, with an odd recognition, in the bar last night.

Shit.

"Alex!" I look over with dread to where the door has just re opened. The nameless blonde that I hoped I would never see again is marching towards me and the woman I fell for a lifetime ago. She kisses me before I can find my senses, and as I refocus, I watch Ruby's face darken before she turns and walks away.

Sam

"Hey Ruby, what's your poison?" As I notice my old friend, I see her face and feel a tension that I can't find the source of.

Ruby looks at me as if I've just thrown her a lifeline, and I point to a multitude of alcohol with a smile as she all but runs to meet me at the bar.

"Wine please" She says, the wave of her hand points to a bottle of Merlot on the shelf, so I reach for a glass.

"So you saw Alex is working here?" Her expression tells me she wishes she'd had notice from me earlier.

"He seems to have settled in with the locals, how long has he been here?" She looks over at Alex with something between scorn and longing. I should really find out what happened when she left.

"Maybe six months, but it's been a rough ride. Have you not talked to him?" I place the large glass of red in front of her, which she takes a grateful long sip of.

"To be honest Sam, I've been off the radar; I lost my phone when I went travelling. It's only when I ran into you that I realised how much I'd missed everyone" Her eyes connect with mine again, and she gives me a weak smile.

"Well, I for one am glad your back. Millie

should be here any minute so you won't be drinking alone" My attempt to cheer her up seems to go unnoticed as she turns back to where Alex's blonde friend is clinging onto him. He looks a bit lost as he gestures over to me and heads into the staff room. Ruby catches my eye as he walks past and raises her eyebrows.

"Alex doesn't quite seem himself. What's he been doing?"

"I'm guessing you want a different answer than 'that blonde'?" I deliver the question with less tact than I could have, but it makes me giggle. It has a different effect on Ruby.

"I didn't think Amy would be his type" she says, with something close to disappointment in her voice.

As I wonder how to respond, Millie's face appears at the window and bursts through the door towards us.

Alex

"Ruby - wait!" I've kept my distance all night, but I can't let her leave without at least trying to make amends.

"What do you want?" She turns around, taking in my unwashed hair and what must be dilated pupils. I really should start using mirrors for more than self-deprecation again.

"I'm sorry about Amy" is all that I can think to say.

"Why are you sorry, Alex? Who you sleep with is none of my business "She looks up at me with those amazing eyes, warm and deep as chocolate. Her hair, somehow the same colour, but cascading from her shoulders and making me want to run my fingers through it.

"I didn't realise you were friends, and it was just a onetime thing. The last few months have been a bit of a blur, and I didn't expect to see you" I use a cloth to wipe down a table, so I have something to do with my hands.

"Alex, what's going on with you? "Ruby sits down at the table, and looks at me with concern. Somehow in one small sentence, she has reminded me that she's the only person since Kate who's been able to break through all my barriers.

I sit down opposite her, start to form words and feel my throat tighten. My whole life is a mess, and has been since this one person left me alone in it.

Kate was my partner for a long time, but I've never known anyone else like Ruby. She can seem to know what I'm thinking without me opening my mouth, and she was important enough for me to throw away the only love that I'd ever had. I look up at her and tears fill my eyes. I hang my head and cover it with my hands. Ruby had seen me at my lowest a few years ago, when Kate had shown her true colours, but she had no idea how much lower rock bottom had become since she'd left. I was left to fend for myself without anyone who had cared about me, only to realise that I didn't care about myself anymore. Now that she was sat in front of me again, all I wanted to do was to pour my heart out into hers without uttering a word.

"Alex?" She whispers, reaching out a hand to brush the hair gently from my face. I take a deep breath, wondering how to put the last year into words.

"I don't know, Ruby. I don't know what I'm doing. I've messed everything up, and I can't seem to sort myself out", I make eye contact with her, and suddenly manage to say, "I miss you" before I feel the sting of tears behind my eyelids again.

I feel her eyes on me as I release my head onto my hands and tremble as more tears spill out. I can imagine her face wincing uncomfortably as she watches me unravel, not knowing what to say to this drunken stranger whom she used to know so well. It takes me a while to centre myself and gather the courage to meet her eyes again. When I do, all I see is the beautiful face of my best friend full of love and concern. She gives a sad smile and says four words that I'd hoped for but hadn't expected.

"I miss you too."

Millie

I'm coming to realise that it's been too long since I had alcohol.

In the past few months since the shop was legally mine and the labourers finished their work, I've been working all hours trying to get things straight and make sure that my Nan's money is put to good use. I've been so nervous to get everything right that even Sam has struggled to make me take the odd night off. I've tried to do this, but inevitably have ended up falling asleep while she and Ben watch a film. Working so hard has been a vicious cycle of ambition and loneliness, but I'm determined that now it's ready to open that things will be easier to balance.

I stand up from the booth, waiting for Sam to finish cleaning tables. I'd wondered where Ruby had disappeared to, but the answer appears as I turn towards the door. I see Ruby and Alex in an embrace so private that I feel wrong for watching. Alex looks drunk and distraught, clinging onto Ruby as she sits beside him and holds him. As I decide to turn away, Ruby shifts and I catch her eye, a sad smile crosses her lips. Sam walks over to me, a puzzled look on her face as she sees what I see.

"I've never understood their friendship" is all she says as she settles in the seat opposite me.

"They were always close, maybe just catching up?" I venture, though Sam's face paints a different picture.

"Well, I don't know. I'm having real problems with him though" she looks at me with a fixed gaze, my best friend in need of some advice.

"What kind of problems?" I ask, wanting to help if I can.

"I'm a bit conflicted Millie, if it was anyone else I'd have sacked him by now" I realise now that I've not talked to her about this before. I've been in my own ambitious little bubble.

"He turns up to work late and sometimes drunk, but I've tried to talk to him and he won't listen to me. He's our friend Millie and he needs help. What do I do?" Sam has asked me about staff issues before, but I've never known her manage a friend. I look outside at two old friends supporting each other, while one is openly sobbing with his back to us.

"I wouldn't usually say this, but maybe talk to Ruby. If he'll confide in anyone, it's her and she could help both of you" I look across at Sam, who's watching the scene outside. She chews on her thumbnail, and frowns slightly. I wonder if she's frustrated that she's taken time to help out a friend who won't let her in, but can see him opening up completely to someone who's been out of his life for so long.

Ruby

I must have been sat outside with my estranged best friend for at least an hour. I'm not sure if that's even the best way to describe him. Alex has been lots of things to me over the last five years, but the relationship I most miss is best friend. We used to make sense of each other's lives before we complicated them.

We've not talked since things changed; I gathered that he and Kate split up when Luke and I did, but it's still such a raw subject, two years on, that I'm not sure if we can talk about it. I'm not sure that Alex can talk about anything just now, as he's been sobbing on my shoulder for a while. I wish I could take away whatever he's been suffering through since I've been gone, but that's not how life works. Maybe now that I'm back, I can help him sort it out, but he seems so vulnerable. I try to absorb some of his pain by holding him, willing him to cry so that he lets it out. As he cries, my gaze drifts to where Sam and Millie are sat watching us. Millie looks sympathetic, but there is something in Sam's eyes that makes me feel guilty for showing an old friend some affection.

It's clear that Alex has been causing Sam some problems since he's been working for her. Even from what I've witnessed tonight, I'm fairly sure that Alex hasn't finished his shift but has spent a lot of it with me (while no other customers have been sat outside) but all I've tried to do is offer a shoulder and give him the comfort that he obviously needs. I move my eye line from the uncomfortable line of Sam's and shift slightly so that Alex lifts his head from my shoulder. He looks up at me with an unreadable expression, and clears his throat.

"I'm sorry, I shouldn't have done that" He suddenly stands and turns away from me, his hands running through his hair in a gesture so familiar to me that the last two years vanish.

"Alex, it's ok. You don't have to apologise to me" I stand up, trying to bring him back to the intimacy that we've always had.

"I should, I should be doing lots of things and I'm failing. I should be able to talk to an old friend without losing it, and I shouldn't even be sat out here. I'm working, I need to go and help Sam-"As he turns back towards the bar, I catch his hand and keep it in mine.

"Alex, it's ok. We'll make it all ok" I say to him, not knowing what else to say but enjoying how his hand feels at home in mine.

"How? "His eyes look deep into mine; searching for the person he used to know.

"I don't know, but we always made sense of things together. I'm sorry that I left before and left you to try and figure things out alone. I'm back now; can't we go back to how it was?" As soon as I say this, I remember how it was between us, and realise this wasn't the best line. I suddenly wonder how many times Sam re filled my wine glass.

"You want to go back to how it was?" He keeps his eyes on mine but his expression changes to something I can't fathom. Surprise perhaps? Or something closer to attraction.

"I want to go back to when we were friends and made sense of things together" I watch as the unreadable expression shifts from his face, but less than a second later, it's replaced with a smile.

"I'd like that" He says, his eyes breaking contact and moving to Sam who is starting to look angry inside the bar. He gives me an apologetic smile and goes back inside.

Alex

It's been a week since Ruby came back, and we've decided to meet for a drink. I didn't want Sam watching over us, so we're going to a pub near the train station that we went to on that fateful night when everything fell apart. I admit that I suggested this pub to stir up some old memories, because nothing in my life has ever made sense like it did when Ruby and I got drunk and put the world to rights.

I look into the bedroom mirror as I get ready and realise that this is the first time that Ruby and I will be drinking together with no one waiting at home for either of us. It shouldn't, but that thought makes my heart beat a bit faster as I change my shirt and spray some after shave.

I'd promised myself last week that I wouldn't drink too much, but the thought of catching up properly with Ruby has brought out my nerves so I make my way into the kitchen and the corner cupboard that has for the past year homed my emergency alcohol. I take a moderate swig of vodka, a deep breath and a last thought of self-hatred before moving towards the door.

As I'd expected, Ruby doesn't arrive until I've found us a secluded booth and bought us both a glass of the red wine that she'd chosen in the Night Light last week. I'm watching the door, not sure that she'll turn up, when I see her across the street and she takes my breath away. Dressed in skinny jeans and a low cut black top, her face alone takes me back to a time when retail therapy and a glass of wine would help me through the day. As I watch her, she looks up and catches my eye. Her easy smile makes me feel guilty for needing my usual few shots of confidence before leaving the flat, but my heartbeat jumps when she opens the door and I know that I need all the strength I can get not to screw this friendship up again.

"Hey, trouble" She leans in to kiss me on the cheek and I smell her perfume – the same that she wore before. It brings a warm smile to my face that she returns as she sits opposite me. I push her wine towards her, which she takes with a grateful grin, and looks around at the pub with barely contained nostalgia. I hope she hasn't noticed my plan.

"We've been here before, it's lovely" She says as she settles into the sofa. The pub has changed hands in the last few years, but the rustic, ambient atmosphere remains. There are now stairs next to the bar that lead up to an area with more sofas and a section where local bands come to play acoustic sets. I've been here a few times in the last year, in my contemplative moods, and each time I've thought of Ruby and how she would love it.

"It's one of my favourite places" I tell her, not

adding that it reminds me of her. I sip at my wine, wary that I need to pace myself.

"So, how were your travels?" I ask, regretting immediately where I know this question will lead.

"Come on, surely Amy shared all of our stories with you? What else did you two talk about after sex?" She asks with that cheeky look that I remember well, and I know I should have asked something else.

"OK, message received. I will never again sleep with someone you know. Though, in my defence, I only have a very hazy recollection of that night" I give her a sheepish grin, which makes her laugh and suddenly breaks any tension at the table.

We talk for hours, and manage to somehow get back to the easy companionship that made us so close before. I'm not sure whether Ruby can sense it whenever she makes me nervous, but I'm determined not to ruin this night. I lost her once by being drunk and foolish, and I'll do everything I can not to lose her again.

Ruby

I'm not sure what I was scared of, but tonight is just what I remembered of Alex. We seem to fit, regardless of context or circumstance. Maybe that's what best friends are – people who can go for years without contact and meet up as if no time has passed.

I sit across the table from him, my second glass of wine almost empty, and smile at him. He seems different tonight, more in control of himself than when I saw him at the Night Light. Maybe it's just because no one is watching us, but it feels like old times. He catches my smile and raises an eyebrow.

"What?" He asks, innocently nursing his glass.

"Nothing, just feels weird to have gone so long without seeing you" I say, draining the last of my wine and placing the glass onto the table between us.

"So, what happened with Kate in the end?" I ask, watching his face to see if this is too sore a subject.

"Oh God . . . Everything happened. We realised we were in two different places and it wasn't fair for either of us. Not sure it's a good subject after a few glasses of wine. Do you want another refill?" He gestures to my empty glass, and although I start to shake my head he nods and brings out another giggle from our former drinking days. He was always such a bad influence, but I'm not ready to end the night yet.

The thought of the good old days conjures up images of Alex sleeping on my sofa, which reminds me that I've got a similar fate ahead of me for a while until I can find work and figure out somewhere to rent. This makes me glad that I'd opted for the extra glass; my temporary sofa is in Sam's boyfriend's flat. As grateful as I am for the hospitality, I'm not too keen to walk back into a boy's flat when they're bound to be having another house party full of strangers.

"What's with the sad face?" Alex asks as he hands me my drink.

"Not sad, just wondering how you so happily slept on a sofa for so long" I say with a half laugh.

"You're sleeping on someone's sofa?" He asks, his face softening in concern as he sees me rub at my neck.

"I know, not the most glamorous of beds, but I'm low on options recently" I take a long sip of wine.

"So, why not come and stay with me? "His face turns serious with the question. I raise my eyebrows as I look up at him. He sees my expression and chuckles quietly.

"I'm serious; the sofa folds out into a bed and

it'll be a hell of a lot more comfortable than a normal futon. I'll even close the bedroom door if the snoring is a problem" His laugh is infectious and I wonder if this is a good idea.

"Are you sure it won't be weird?" I ask once the laughter has subsided.

"How will it be weird?" He asks, taking another gulp of wine.

"Are you forgetting the past few years, and what came before that?"

"Ruby, that was a long time ago, and I think we've both changed. I fell apart on you last week, and I'm sorry. I missed my best friend and now she's here and needs my help. Forgive me for trying to help you" I look into his eyes and see the Alex that I used to know. Maybe it's not such a bad idea, and it can't be worse than a flat with three students.

"It may be the extra glass of wine, but that would be lovely Alex, thank you" I smile and wonder what I'm getting myself into and if all the history we have can stay in the past.

Alex

I wake up suddenly and wonder what's wrong.

Something's different.

I'm in my own bed, and I can feel the sunlight on my face before I open my eyes. I must not have closed the curtains, but that's not what's bringing me this odd and unsettled feeling.

Am I late for work? I glance at the clock – 11.23 – No work for hours. I try to clear my head and that's when I realise.

My head isn't hurting, and I don't feel sick.

There have been several days recently when I've woken up like this, and it feels a bit peculiar, in a good way of course. I have spent a lot of the last few years with my head in the sand, trying to stop the past from filtering through. Obviously this hasn't worked and I need to sort myself out before the need for rehab or complete self-destruction enters the equation.

With a clear head, I shower and change before walking through to wake Ruby. As I open the door, I see her huddled under a blanket on the fold out sofa: A wave of affection flows through me as I watch her sleep. Her face is a picture of innocence, and her nose is scrunched up in a dream that brings a cute intimacy to her face I realise I've never seen before.

I decide to try and walk past her towards the

kitchen, remembering that she needs caffeine for her faculties to kick in. I fill up the kettle and can't stop myself from turning to watch her face while the water boils.

It's true that I fell in love with her a long time ago, at a most inappropriate time, and the way I dealt with that ruined everything. It's a miracle that she found her way back into my life, much less onto my sofa. Now I have a clear head, I realise that I'm lucky to have regained her friendship, and can't let that go.

Ruby

Why is someone playing guitar loudly while I sleep?

I pull the pillow over my head to drown out the noise, only for a random hand to accost my face.

"Ruby?" A familiar voice is whispering, but it still doesn't explain the guitars. I let the pillow get moved aside, but resolve to be grumpy to whoever is to blame. My eyes adjust and see Alex sat on the floor, his hand brushing hair from my eyes. He hands me my phone, which I realise is the thing responsible for the loud guitar noise.

I attempt a hello, but it comes out as a muffled groan as I bring myself up to sit and wonder how the time on my phone reads 12.03

"What time did we get back?" I ask, my head feeling a little sore.

"Not too late, maybe 1?" He replies, gesturing for me to give him room on the sofa while he puts a steaming mug of coffee in front of me. I oblige, not enjoying the way that my head pounds at the movement.

"What? Travelling didn't teach you to drink more than a few?" He glances at me sideways, and through my mind's fog I can see the Alex I used to know. There's something cheeky in his demeanour, and a smile that could melt the hardest heart.

"Are you working today?" I ask him, wanting to change the subject.

"Not until 6. You?"

"Another day of job hunting, though Amy asked if I'd meet her for lunch" I watch his reaction to this, and he grimaces slightly whilst avoiding my eye.

"Well, have fun with that. I'm not sure she's quite forgiven me for not returning her calls" His sigh becomes a small chuckle, so I slap him gently.

"I've never known you as this single heartbreaker Alex; I'm not sure about it. Amy liked you a lot" I chide him with a smile.

"Really? Well, she seemed to like a few other blokes at the Night Light when you came back. Forgive me for not losing any sleep over that one" My smile stays in place, knowing that Amy is anything but the relationship type.

"Fair play my friend. Do you mind if I use your shower before I go?" I drain the last of my coffee and look around for my bag.

"Of course, and you can stay here as long as you need to Ruby, honestly" He pulls my bra from under the blanket and hands it to me, his cheeks blushing a little.

"You're enjoying having a girl's underwear in your lounge?" We both laugh, and I head through to the bathroom before the blush reaches my cheek.

Sam

"Hey gorgeous" Ben's voice accompanies a quiet knock on my bedroom door.

It's my day off, and I've not long woken up. I'd got as far as underwear and a short denim skirt, choosing a matching green set with lace that Ben bought for me last Valentine's Day. He sees this and I sense the lust in his eyes as he closes the door behind him.

"Morning babe" I turn to him from making the bed, and his fingertips move to trace a rose tattoo on my thigh. He kisses me, his fingers rising to my hips.

"I'd thought we could go into town for some lunch, but I like your idea better" He smiles, kissing my neck as his hands move to unbutton my skirt. My hair grazes my cheek and Ben reluctantly uses a hand to replace the strand behind my ear.

"Nice idea, but I promised Millie that I'd spend an hour handing out flyers for her shop. Want to help me, we can have lunch afterwards? It's a warm day; we could have a picnic in the park" He looks at me and his trademark cheeky look returns.

"You, me, wine and a blanket on the grass? Sounds good" His lips brush mine and he moves to sit down on the bed and I finish getting dressed.

"Hey, did you hear from Ruby this morning? I

don't think she came home last night" His words bring a frown to my face.

"No. I'll text her now, just to check on her" I reach for my bag and retrieve my phone.

"I'm sure she's fine babe, just thought I'd mention it" He smiles at me, unsure whether he should have stayed quiet I'm sure.

"Yeah, she can look after herself I know. Thanks" I pick out a blue top and some sandals and check the time, "Shit, I told Millie I'd be at the shop half an hour ago! Come on darling" I usher him out of the door, grabbing my bag on the way.

Ruby

I feel a bit strange about meeting up with Amy, having not seen her since the night after she slept with Alex. It's not that I'm jealous, but after sharing the story of our friendship with her while we were halfway across the world, I find it unsettling that she felt so comfortable seducing him.

Maybe that's unfair, and maybe he seduced her, but either way I'm intrigued to see how she'll react to me today.

She's flirting with the barman when I walk into the bar. Her hair falling across her shoulders as she twirls a piece around her finger, and giggles at something he's said.

I take a seat on the sofa opposite her, and gesture to him that I'd like a drink if he's spent enough time flirting. I can't say I hadn't noticed this side of Amy when we were travelling, but for some reason it hadn't bothered me when we were in need of foreign friends.

"Hey babe" She gives me a kiss on the cheek; oblivious to the barman's stare as she settles back on the sofa.

"Hey, how have you been?" I take in her sparkly blue eyes and tanned shoulders and see the girl who took me away from confusion and heartache. This girl wasn't malicious; she simply refused to take any part of life seriously, including men.

"Same really: missing travelling as much as I miss my grandpa. Things were simpler on a hammock on an Australian beach" She smiles at me, and I remember how much fun we had.

"That they were" I take my diet coke from the barman with a tired smile. Amy sees this and gives me a confused look as she sips from a cocktail.

"Hung over are we?" She asks.

"Maybe a bit: Alex and I caught up last night and there was wine involved. He seemed fine this morning, but my head is sore" I sip from my drink, enjoying the quiet fizz on my tongue.

"That doesn't surprise me babe, he drinks like a fish! I'm not sure he even remembered me when we woke up together" I catch her eye, but she just shrugs and drinks more of her cocktail. I think back to the other week at the Night Light, how Alex seemed drunk and emotional.

"Have you seen him much since we've been back?" I ask her, concerned.

"Nope, just that one memorable night – Though he never called me so I guess it's onto the next" She sighs, and then smiles as she looks over to the barman.

As we order food, I'm beginning to worry that while I was gone I left my best friend alone when he needed me the most.

Alex

For some reason, the fact that Ruby is meeting Amy makes me uneasy. I never mentioned Ruby to Amy, so my feelings are a bit odd. But somehow, a girl you've slept with being friends with a girl you've loved – requited or otherwise - doesn't seem right: It's almost like your ex's getting together and comparing notes.

It's meant that even though I woke up sober and content this morning, I felt the need to down my usual few shots of vodka before heading out for my shift. This seemed a bad idea once I got to the Night Light and Sam cornered me in the staff room.

"Alex, I think we need to talk before you start" She says, a strange look on her face.

"OK, what? Are you breaking up with me?" I try for a smile, but her eyes tell me that wouldn't go down well.

"I just want to know what's going on with you. You've seemed to be struggling, turning up late, hung over. Then Ruby turns up and you spend half of your shift outside crying to her. I'm not judging you, Alex, and I can give you help if you need it. But I need you to be honest with me" As she speaks, her words seem to bounce off me. I know I need this job, and I try to muster all of my patience as I look at her.

"Sam, I'm sorry. Things have been rough for me but I'm working on it. Ruby took me by surprise, but it's going to be fine now. Please, just give me some time and let me do my job?" I give her a tight smile, which she seems to reciprocate, and walk quickly into the bar area.

Ruby

After seeing Amy yesterday, her new barman friend has invited us to a club night tonight at one of our favourite bars. I'm a bit dubious, but have never been a girl to turn down a night out. I'd have invited Alex, but I'm guessing he won't want to socialise with a former conquest. Plus, he's been asleep for most of the day after getting home from work in a foul mood last night.

I've been back to Ben's flat today to pick up some of my things, and to thank him for his hospitality. He seemed less than thrilled that I was moving out, and was insistent that I could come back if I needed to. I really should talk to Sam and see what's gone on with Alex to wind Ben up so much.

There's a knock at the door as I'm putting the finishing touches to my make up in the lounge mirror. As I reach the hallway, Alex is nearing the door in his pyjama bottoms.

"Can I help you?" He asks to a very cute looking guy, hopefully the barman's friend.

"Hi, yeah, I'm here to pick up Ruby?" There's a vulnerability to his voice, perhaps in response to the sharpness of Alex's tone.

"I'll tell her your here" He gives a humourless laugh and closes the door. As he turns, he sees me and looks me up and down. His eyes take in my dress and heels, and he tries to compose himself.

"What was that?" I ask, expecting an apology.

"Just some random salesman" He replies, walking back towards the lounge. Or, I suppose, my bedroom.

"Alex, is there a problem?" I reach for his hand, but he pulls away from me.

"A problem? That depends, Ruby. I offered you my sofa to sleep on, and a friend to talk to. What I didn't expect was for you to invite random guys over to screw on that sofa" He avoids my eyes, but I can see that his are filling up.

"What? Alex, I'm not planning on screwing anyone. Even if I was, you said it wouldn't be weird when you invited me. What's going on?" I reach for him, but he has already stepped towards his own bedroom.

"Nothing's going on, I just don't like being used that's all" His words are almost lost as he walks away.

I make my apologies to Amy outside, suddenly not in the mood to socialise. She doesn't seem to mind, having both men to choose from now. I, myself, have one to figure out.

I change back into my jeans and an Oasis t-shirt, and wander through to the bedroom.

"What exactly was that about?" I ask him as I stand in the doorway, watching him put on a jumper.

"Leave it, Ruby. Why didn't you go?" He looks up at me, his eyes alighting on my top and smiling at the memory of the gig we both went to where I bought it.

"I didn't go because my best friend is upset, and I thought we could go for a walk instead?" I hold out my hand in a gesture of solidarity and, to my surprise, he walks towards me and puts it in his own.

Alex

We are walking towards the park, and the beauty is not lost on us. The sunset is stunning, and I'm trying to use it as inspiration to say something that I should have said a long time ago.

"So, you want to tell me why you've been acting so weird?" Is the line that Ruby chooses to open the conversation? I take a deep, heavy breath, and try to find the words.

"OK, I'm guessing you probably know this already but I need to say it all before you respond. I've been in love with you for a long time, Ruby. Since before I kissed you all those months ago, and I'm so sorry about how I've gone about things. When you left, I didn't know which way was up and I buried myself in a whirlwind of alcohol and sex. I never should have acted on things with you the way I did, and I'm sorry about how that left things with you and Luke" I ignore the confusion in her beautiful eyes, and try to keep talking.

"When you came back, I had got myself into such a state that just seeing your face sent my world upside down. I thought I had it all under control, but it seems that I was very, very wrong. I can't apologise for falling for you. I won't. But I'm sorry about how horribly I've reacted to it. I'm not expecting you to forgive me, but I don't think it's fair on either of us for me to keep this from you any longer" As I stop, I realise I've been studying the grass beneath us as we've settled on the swings. I'm grateful that the chains are giving my hands something to do, and I take another breath before I dare to raise my head.

As I lift my eyes, I see tears in hers. Whether they are good or bad tears I'm not sure yet, but it's time for her to speak. It must be, it seems like I've been talking for years, and I'm not sure my throat will let any other words through.

"Alex" Is all she says, and she takes my hand as she brings us both to our feet. Frankly, I'm a bit surprised that mine will hold me up.

We wander slowly through the grass, and I follow her lead. The enormity of what I've just said sinks through my skin, and I know that I could have just lost my best friend forever. Where do we go from here?

She pulls me to her, and I take the chance to look her in the eye, in case it is my last. I almost flinch as I feel her fingertips on my cheek: Will she hit me? But no, her touch is gentle, almost tender. She brings my face near enough to her own that I can feel her breath on my cheek. She says my name again, a whisper this time. And then, all of a sudden, her lips brush mine. It is the kiss that I've waited almost two years for, since that moment of weakness on her sofa. A lot of the self-loathing has come from that night – Luke never would have laid a finger on her if I hadn't been so selfish. But I try to ignore all the noise in my head, push it all aside and focus on the inconceivable and amazing fact, that Ruby is kissing me.

Millie

I'm sat in my office, staring at the computer screen and hoping for a miracle.

Ever since opening, I've been tired and busy and wondering if I've got my sums wrong. But, upon cashing up tonight it's becoming clear that I need some kind of help. I'd thought that our little city with a village vibe would be the perfect place to introduce and grow a little craft business. However, I can't keep ignoring that customers just aren't spending enough to make up for my start-up costs.

There's no way I'm giving up what I've worked so hard for – Besides the fact that I will not let my Nan down. There must be something I can do. I run my fingers through my hair and reach for my phone. I scroll through my contacts, hoping to stumble upon someone that I'd forgotten about whose running their own business and can offer some tips. I suddenly almost laugh out loud at the absurdity of the attempt. Instead, I find Sam's number and send a text to request an emergency pub meeting.

As I wait for her to reply, I finish cashing up and sigh at the negative figure on the screen. I shut down the computer, feeling the spreadsheets mocking me as I do so. I lock the door to the small office at the back of the shop, and I look up to see

Sam pulling a comical face at me through the front door. I smile at her, feeling the stress slowly ebbing away from my shoulders as I let her in.

"Bad day?" She asks as she tries on a ring from a display that has silver butterflies decorating the band.

"Not just the day, it's been a bad week Sam. I'm worried that I can't afford to keep things going" I feel tears stinging the back of my eyes as I try to compose myself.

"Don't be silly, Mills. It'll all be fine. I've just left Ben with his friends at the pub at the end of the high street, so why don't we go and have a drink in here?" She gestures to the bar closest to the shop, one that we'd been to frequently during the painting and decorating stage of renovation

Sam buys the drinks while I grab a table at the back of the room. I remember the nights when we would come in here and unwind, hoping the memories will help me to get past this nagging feeling that I've bitten off more than I can chew.

"I believe we need one of these" She says as she places a huge pink cocktail in front of me, complete with an umbrella and – my favourite – a cherry. I laugh at the sight of it.

"What the hell is that?!" I ask, having ordered a Malibu and coke.

"It's an alcoholic stress reliever. The bar lady said it was ladies' night" We look around the bar and see less than a handful of girls, none of them drinking cocktails.

"I think we've found your first lesbian stalker!" I giggle, trying to keep my voice down as the bar lady glances up from the empty bar.

"Oh no, my first lesbian stalker was one of my first customers at the Night Light. She was crazy for tattoos" The cheeky look in Sam's eye keeps my giggles going, even as I try the bubblegum-coloured drink. It actually tastes really good; fruity and very strong. There may even be Malibu in there somewhere.

"Wow, that's gorgeous!" Sam says after a sip, "Maybe I should make Ben aware of my other options?" She winks at me, and then settles back into the seat.

"So, why such a bad day Millie? Can I help, other than with the drinks of course" She looks at me, her smile fading as she prepares to give advice.

"Oh Sam, I'm really struggling. I've been cashing up this last week and the figures just aren't cutting it. I'm worried that I'm not going to be able to sustain this business" As I start to talk, I can feel the tears coming again and drink from the cocktail to stop them breaking free.

"Maybe it's just a quiet patch? It's the summer and people are away on holidays. Do you need help with the figures and maybe advice on keeping costs down and stuff?" She leans forward, biting on her lip.

"Yeah, that would help. But who can do that? You've got management experience, but you have a finance department in the company. How do I do that on my own?" I wipe a tear from my eye and try to think.

"Do you have any friends who are accountants?" She asks in vain.

"Not that I can think of. I can't even think of anyone from University who did anything like that" I meet her eyes, and suddenly hers grow wide.

"What?" I ask, intrigued.

"Didn't Luke do an Accounting degree?" She says, grabbing her phone from her bag.

"Maybe, but I haven't spoken to him since he left" I look at her, confused at how this will help. She shows me her phone.

"That, my dear, is what social networking is for."

Ruby

I feel like I have pins and needles all over.

I'm not sure how Alex and I got back from the park to his flat, but we have been sat on the floor of his lounge for hours. We have talked ourselves in circles, recounting the last few years and the things that we'd missed out on. But there's a whole other layer, a layer that I'd not thought could ever be possible.

Everyone's had that feeling of exhilaration at the start of a relationship, when every touch brings a rush of excitement. I had that feeling with Luke, right from the start. But, I've never had that feeling with someone that I already know. There's an extra dimension of safety with Alex, especially after the speech he gave me at the park. I don't understand how someone that I've held and touched a million times is suddenly giving me goose bumps. If I think about it too much, I'm sure the feeling will go away, so I get up to peruse his CD collection.

"Bored of Elbow are we?" He asks, kissing mine and smiling.

"Not yet, just getting the next album ready" I run my fingertips along the shelves, enjoying that I can remember when most of these CDs were bought. I hesitate by Aerosmith, Kings of Leon and Oasis before alighting on Red Hot Chili Peppers and holding it up for approval.

"It's my collection, you can choose what you wish" He says, laughing at my sudden uncertainty. He looks at the clock on the wall.

"Though, it's past two. Aren't you tired?" I shake my head, yawning as I do so. His smile is more affectionate now, his fingers finding mine and playing with them.

"I wondered if you might be ready for an upgrade from the sofa to my bed?" His voice is thick now, though with tiredness or lust I'm not sure.

I can't pretend that I'm not excited at the prospect, but it still feels a bit alien. This is Alex, my best friend, who is suddenly becoming so much more than that. His hand touches my hip and turns me towards the bedroom. As soon as I get to the doorway though, he pulls me back towards him as if I was too far away for that short walk. His kiss starts gently, but with each second it becomes more urgent, passionate. I pull away slightly, wanting to see his face. He's smiling; the smile that comes from his eyes and teases me as he leans in for another kiss. He bites my lip gently, his hands grabbing my hair before moving my t shirt aside to caress the skin of my stomach. He pulls the top over my head, looking into my eyes to question as a last resort whether I'm ready for what's about to happen. I smile slowly, my hands already pulling at his clothes as the Cast of

Thousands album comes to an end and we begin to make our own music.

Millie

Ok, I'm now feeling completely out of my depth.

I've lost count of the amount of times during my friendship with Sam that I've felt like I'm in her shadow. She's prettier, more street wise and more confident. She's always been the outspoken and interesting one, with men and women alike always wanting to hear about her many tattoos and whatever crazy stories she has from gigs or boyfriends. I've never resented her, purely because I love her. She's my best friend and we've been through a lot together, but days like this one still bring out my inferiority complex.

We are at home, and are sprawled on the sofa with her laptop in between us. She has opened Facebook and is showing me her profile. I've never been on a website like this before, and it's looking a bit overwhelming.

"You know, you can make a page for businesses and post information and photos. It might help you to promote the shop and get more people to know about it" She's clicking on lots of different things, which is starting to give me a headache.

"OK, maybe that can be a lesson for another day. So, how do we look for Luke?" I'm watching as she types his name into the search bar, and suddenly a list of names and faces are looking out at us. The second face is Luke's and Sam smiles at me.

"Awesome, he's on it. See, not everyone's a technophobe like you!" She laughs and clicks a button that says 'send friend request'.

"So, we just wait for him to confirm and then we can ask for his advice and see if he's still living nearby" She says smugly, as she checks her own page for messages or comments or whatever she does on here. There are lots of photos of her (and me, I suddenly realise) and bands who have played at the Night Light.

"OK. So, you use this to promote the bar as well as posting your unassuming friends up for the world to see?" I catch her eye, sticking out my tongue so she knows I'm not really offended.

"Yep, it's great. Head office wants to give each bar a page of their own, but they were happy for me to gauge interest through my page first. They saw that I had a lot of friends on here, which is more than I'd have on a new page obviously" As she explains it to me, I look where she points on the menu bar and see that she has over 200 friends. She's always been something of a social butterfly, but 200? If I made a page, I'd be lucky to break 50. I comment on this and she laughs.

"I started out about a year ago, and I had about 50 friends for months. Gradually, people that you meet look for you on here. It's all a bit odd, but I love taking photos so it's dead easy once you get the hang of it" She clicks a few more buttons before I've had enough and get up to put the kettle on.

"Not a fan?" She asks, giggling at my impatience. Since I only had a camera phone when Sam gave me her old one, she's aware of how rubbish I am with things like this.

"Not really, but if Luke can help with the shop then I promise I'll have a look and try out the extra promotion. Deal?" I ask as I set a steaming mug of tea in front of her.

"Deal, but only if you didn't finish the biscuits?" She holds out her hand as I drop a chocolate digestive into it, and she smiles.

Wow.

It's been a really long time since I had this feeling. You know that amazing, scary feeling that you get when you wake up next to someone for the first time after everything has changed? Maybe it's just me, but I've always been the kind of girl who needs to know someone before sex and relationships comes into play. I perhaps have trust issues, or maybe my standards are just a bit higher than all of my friends who had at least their fair share of one night stands throughout getting our degrees.

I never saw the appeal of letting someone I'd just met share the most personal thing you can give to them. With Luke, we were housemates for a while first, and there was a lot of flirting, but we both knew that we wanted a relationship when we got together. After things ended so abruptly there, it was a slight shock to the system to see Amy in action in unfamiliar surroundings: She had always been, shall we say, wild. She'd not had a relationship longer than a few months during University, and I'd heard a lot of different names batted around. I had a lot to figure out while we travelled, hence my need to go in the first place, but I still think she was disappointed that I wouldn't take her advice to 'have fun' as she put it, and join her in relishing the travelling experience by sleeping with all the locals. It did give her free reign though, which she was fine with, but I feel guilty having left her alone last night. I decide to see if she wants a morning after chat, as I don't expect Alex to wake up for a while yet.

I get up from the crumpled sheets, and look around for my clothes. My jeans are lying on the floor, and I reach for them as I locate my t shirt under the pillow. I've left my dressing gown at Ben's, but decide that I need a shower. I glance at Alex, his face pretty and vulnerable as he sleeps.

I shower quickly, before remembering that my clean underwear is in my bag in the lounge. I pad through the bedroom in the tiny towel, and Alex is awake, sitting on the edge of the bed. The sheets are pooled in his lap, patches of his skin just visible amongst the black.

"Morning" I say to him with a smile as I move to walk past him.

"Good morning" He doesn't let me past, but tries to coax me back into bed with his feet and hands.

"Alex, I need my clothes" I giggle, enjoying the slightly odd feeling of being so connected to him.

"No you don't, what good will clothes do?" He asks, his lips tracing a line across my collarbone as his hand reaches up to my breast, the towel falling away.

"I can't do this when you're dressed" He gently caresses my skin, sending a shiver through my body. He kisses me, and the emotions from last night become more vivid again. He looks into my eyes, his mouth forming a lazy smile as he pulls me on top of him. I steady myself by putting my hands on his shoulders, and as I settle I sense his excitement. His eyes stay locked on mine as he moves to join with me once again.

"Are you happy?" He asks, his pupils already having dilated slightly. He supports my lower back as we ease into a slow rhythm.

I answer him with a smile and a long, deep kiss that makes him groan softly. Any plans for the morning have pleasantly slipped from my mind, as I relish this new waking up routine.

Sam

I stand in the lounge, looking at my outfit in the mirror. Millie has actually given in and agreed to come with me to get my new tattoo – She's always been wary of the idea, but she seems to be fascinated whenever I come back from having some new ink. I told her that I was happy to go alone, being good friends with my tattooist by now, but she has insisted.

She walks through from the kitchen with a piece of paper in her hand. As she hands it to me, I see a small heart outline interlocking with a larger one.

"What's this?" I look at her, puzzled.

"I phoned the tattoo shop and asked if I could book a slot next to yours" She smiles cheekily.

"You're having a tattoo?!" I ask, stunned. Millie and I have been best friends for years now, and she's never said she wanted one before.

"Yep, I wanted to design it in secret and surprise you. That's why I was so adamant to come with you!" Her smile is infectious, but I feel a sisterly need to make sure she's sure about what we're about to do.

"Millie, I'm happy to do this, but you do realise that it will be forever? You can't just get rid of it without a scar" I look at her, and she frowns.

"I think I worked that out Sam, thanks. I've

always had a mild curiosity and this is only a little tattoo for my ankle" She matches my sisterly look until I giggle.

I look down at her to see that she has prepared for this by painting her toes and opting for a short but flowing blue skirt with leggings and little blue and white spotty pumps. My plan for the day is to get the outline of butterflies coloured in as they flutter up from the small of my back to my neck. Even though I'm well versed in being tattooed, I still get actual butterflies on the way to the shop. It'll be nice to have Millie there, and quite exciting to be there for her having her first tattoo.

"Ok, ready?" She shares my look of scared excitement as we gather up our bags and head towards the door.

Millie

It's so odd, but after years of curious but scared fascination with Sam's array of tattoos (she says she lost count after about twenty) once I decided to take the plunge, I became quite excited about today.

We're sat in the small but welcoming reception area, waiting for Dan – the tattooist – to finish with his current client. I'm nearest to the doorway, and can see the person who is in the chair: A man in his late twenties, with not much skin left to put ink on from what I can see. Dan is holding the needle to the man's throat, colouring a skull in green. The sight makes me look across to Sam, who giggles and holds my gaze for a moment.

I continue to look around the reception area at the vast array of pictures displayed as inspiration – Endless artwork from small sugar skulls and dragonflies, up to more crude and large drawings of gothic scenes and warriors. The girl on reception is stunningly beautiful with long, flowing hair that seems to incorporate every colour of the rainbow. She's dressed in faded jeans and a black skinny tee that shows a peek at a colourful array of ink on her toned midriff. She catches my eye, and though she smiles politely, I feel embarrassed to have been caught staring and return my attention to the wall.

I spot one particular framed sketch of what appears to be a severed mermaid's head hanging from a metal spike. Sam must see my reaction, as she touches my arm and covers her mouth to mask a snort of laughter.

"Changing your mind?" She asks, but I shake my head. I'm glad that I chose a small design though.

"Ok, Sean. That's it" Dan says, laughing as the man cheers, then winces at the pain.

"Yeah, it'll be sore for a while, but I think we're almost there!?" Again he laughs; soothing Sean's throat with cream and then gently wrapping it in cling film. Sean grunts and stands up, walking through to the reception area. He pays for the sitting and gives Dan a weird, manly secret handshake before walking through the front door with a pained smile in our direction.

"So Sam, What's the plan for today?" Dan looks up with an almost devilish grin.

"I want to finish my butterflies please, just some greens and blues and some other pretty colours maybe?" Sam stands up and begins to peruse the pictures of designs that line the walls.

"Sounds good, nice choice" He says, and then looks across to me.

"And what about your lovely lady friend?" I feel my cheeks flush, and will myself to be confident.

"Ah, this is Millie. She's here for her first one. I think she booked in for after me, but it's such a small design I'll let her go first if you like?" She looks to me, and I surprise myself by nodding enthusiastically.

"OK then Millie, welcome. Any friend of Sam's is more than welcome, and I'm honoured to be the first!" He gives me a cheeky wink and leans forward as I show him the design.

"Thanks . . . It's only a small one, as Sam said. On my ankle here, please" I gesture to the inside of my left ankle.

"Of course, that looks fairly simple. A good idea to keep the first one small, I'd say. Do you want any colours?" He asks, looking at me with a gentle seriousness.

"Just black I think?" I look up at him, taking in his plethora of ink. It's quite mesmerising when you look at it closely.

"Fair enough, should only take fifteen minutes or so, and then we can crack on with Sam's butterflies" He gives a quick smile before taking the paper from me.

"Take a seat and I'll get the stencil done" He gestures back to my seat, and I oblige, suddenly feeling the nerves take hold.

I take a deep breath and look towards the large window that looks out onto the high street. I watch shoppers stumbling around with their bags and realise that I can see quite far from here.

My gaze falls upon two familiar faces, smiling and laughing amongst themselves. Alex and Ruby are walking down the hill towards the shops.

"Hey, look Sam" I nudge her and we look towards our friends. After watching for a few seconds, I see that they are holding hands, their fingers entwined.

"Are they . . .?" Sam asks, not quite sure how to finish the sentence. The question is answered as Alex pulls Ruby towards him and they share a kiss. A smile follows the kiss, the kind of kiss that you only share with someone you've been naked with. There's an intimacy in their eyes, so much so that we look away, uncomfortable to be intruding on their privacy.

"Well, I guess that's why she's not been staying at Ben's flat!" Sam says: her eyes wide but a smile on her lips.

"Do you think it's a new thing?" I ask, feeling a bit odd even hinting that it's not.

"What do you mean?" She looks at me, puzzled.

"Just that they've known each other for years, do you not think it's strange that they would only just realise if they were attracted to each other?"

"Ruby told me that she hadn't seen him since

she left, and I doubt that she'd lie. Besides, that's the kind of look that couples have right at the start" She gives me a knowing smile and stands back up to join Dan as he returns to the desk.

"Right then Millie, all ready to go?" He rubs his hands mockingly with that devilish grin again, and I laugh and follow him through to the next room.

Alex

It turned out, after offering Ruby a post coital breakfast, that I had no food in the fridge. I appeased her by bringing her into town for brunch.

There's a cafe in the middle of Winchester high street that makes the best bacon and egg sandwiches I've ever had, and I was quite glad that Ruby had never been there. It seemed right after she gave me one of the best nights of my life that I could offer her a new experience in return.

I open the cafe door and let her pass in front of me, relishing how comfortable we are with each other this morning. When I first awoke to hear her in the shower, I'll admit that a mild sense of panic rose in my chest. As soon as I saw her, though, that contented warmth returned and I saw in her smile that the day would be a good one.

She's studying the menu, but I know that we'll both opt for the legendary sandwiches that I've told her about on the walk down from the train station. We place our order and Ruby finds us a table at the back. The chairs are all mismatched and have vintage style upholstery. I'm not surprised that Ruby jumps onto a polka dot chair, while I settle into one with a soft green material.

"These had better be good" She winks at me, looking around at the walls adorned in posters for local music events.

"Trust me, you won't be disappointed" I return her smile and nod at the waitress who brings our plates.

"Wow, I love your dress!" Ruby exclaims, looking in awe at the waitress who's wearing a mint green dress covered in tiny black hearts.

"Thanks hun, my friend has just opened a shop at the other end of the high street – The Purple Penguin? You should have a look" Ruby looks excited, and I know we'll be shopping next. We add sauce and then I watch her face as she takes the first bite. I hate to say, but the face she pulls brings back memories of the last twelve hours.

"Oh wow!" She whispers, wiping a few crumbs from her lips, "OK, I agree, this is definitely worth the train journey" I chuckle as we continue to eat, loving that I'm making her happy with something so simple.

Sam

I lie down on the newly sanitised dentist – style chair and breathe through the excitement.

Millie is sat on a stool next to me, her ankle wrapped up and looking tender. She actually dealt with it well, holding my hand and looking away but talking through the pain. Her hearts took about ten minutes, but it might take Dan a bit longer to colour in my back.

"OK, I just need to sort out the ink. While I'm gone, if you can undo your top and make yourself comfortable?" Dan makes himself scarce, always keen to be a gentleman. I dressed in a backless wrap around top, anticipating this moment, so I untie the bow at the bottom of my back and fold over onto my front. As I shuffle to find a good position to lie still for an hour or two, Millie catches my eye.

"Don't you feel a bit weird, being topless in front of him?" She asks, and I shrug.

"He's a tattooist Mills, he's seen much more than this, and anyway it's only my back he'll see" She watches as I try to stop myself from smiling, remembering whereabouts Dan has tattooed me before.

"OK, point taken", I say, not needing her to verbalise it, "I've had ink in a lot of places, but never anywhere as private as your thinking!" I almost throw my cushion at her, but Dan reappears so I make myself comfortable.

"Right then, all ready?" He smiles as I nod, and he points to the tray that he's carried in.

"So, I thought I'd bring in a rainbow of colours and we could decide as we go along. How many butterflies do we have to colour in?" He glances at the outlines that he finished a few months ago.

"Twelve?" I nod again, and look down at the tray. There's a jade green, a few shades of blue, a deep pink and black.

"I love them, maybe a few butterflies with each colour, and one or two of the smaller ones black?" He looks happy with that, so I try to relax, enjoying the anticipation. He sprays on the cleaning fluid and I wait for the noise of the needle to start up.

Ruby

After perhaps the most amazing sandwich I've ever had, I manage to convince Alex to accompany me to the Purple Penguin.

It reminds me of the days when the two of us would shop before work, but the shop holds a similar kind of excitement to that which Alex and I have seemed to personify in the last twenty-four hours. The owner, who looks the same age as us, welcomes us warmly as we enter. Alex points out the dress that the waitress wore and then smiles as I'm drawn to almost everything else as well.

The shop is small, but doesn't seem poky. There are several racks of dresses, skirts and tops in various styles and colours – most of which are begging me to try them on. I can hear faint, sultry jazz music playing and look over to see that Alex has given in to this and is swaying slightly to the beat.

I walk through the array of clothes and accessories, feeling a dream-like happiness seeping through my skin. Alex seems to be enjoying the new found intimacy and keeps walking up behind me to wrap a hand around my waist or kiss my neck. He allows me to try a few dresses on without following me in, and then meets me at the till as I'm chatting to the owner.

I've been good and only chosen one dress – A

short black floaty dress covered in aqua stars. As I pay, I peruse the notice board on the wall, and spot an advert for a music reviewer. It seems an odd thing to see in a shop like this so I ask the owner about it.

"Oh, my friend put that up. He's worked for the University's magazine for a while but they're struggling to find a decent person to write for local gigs. Weird really, who wouldn't want that job?" She smiles at me as she hands me back my debit card. I make a point to ask for the contact details for the job before we leave.

"How awesome would that be? I'm probably not even qualified, but worth asking, don't you think?" Alex agrees with a smile and a kiss as we amble our way back up the high street.

Millie

I can't help myself, I keep stealing a glance at my foot and the exciting new design that I will forever have there.

For years, the idea of something so permanent was scary, but being here and seeing Dan and his fellow tattooists work I feel proud to have the small hearts adorning my skin.

Sam is about halfway through her session, but is obviously really used to the pain. She has been constantly chatting to Dan and me, only rarely stopping to take a few deep breaths. As she's laughing with Dan about something Ben's done, I hear the familiar chirrup of her phone. I reach into her bag and see that it's a message from Luke.

"What is it Mills?" Sam looks up, trying not to move as she's almost topless.

"It's Luke, should I read it?" I ask, holding her phone so she can see.

"Yes please, it is for you after all" I navigate through the phone menu until I get to the right screen. I touch Luke's message and it appears in a larger form.

Hey Sam – Long time no see! Hope you and Millie are well? I've been back at home for a while now, but freelance work might bring me back down south soon. Maybe we could meet up if your still there? Luke x

"Awesome! We can meet up with him and ask if he could do some extra freelance work for you?!" She smiles, and I put away her phone.

Her optimism is infectious, unless that's just the post ink glow, but either way I touch a finger to the tender skin on my ankle and hope that this is where things will get better for me and my little shop.

Alex

It's been a week now since Ruby and I became a couple, and I still find myself wondering if it's real. I wake up and see her face, all cute and crumpled in sleep, and wonder what I've done to deserve her.

Things have been better at work, mainly because I haven't felt the need to down a bottle of vodka before starting a shift. Sam seems to be happier with me, though has made it clear that if things go downhill again I'll be on thin ice. I have an odd but pleasant feeling that things are finally on the way up.

Ruby's phone starts to ring and she moans into her pillow before reaching for the phone. She talks in a muffled voice for a few seconds, and then suddenly becomes more animated. She thanks the caller and then turns to me with a smile that I feel spread across my own face.

"Good morning" She whispers first, kissing me and leaning in for a cuddle.

"Good news?" I ask, absently tracing my fingertips along her shoulder.

"That was Joe – The guy I emailed about the music reviewer job? He wants me to meet him this afternoon!" She's beaming, and then suddenly giggles as my fingers caress her ticklish elbow.

"That's great news, what time?" I look at the

clock as it blinks 10.04.

"He said 4pm, so I have all day to get ready" She turns around and leans into the curve of my neck. I begin to stroke the soft skin of her back, knowing it's her weakness.

"Get ready? Wouldn't you rather celebrate getting an interview first?" I ask gently in her ear, my lips starting to follow my finger's path. I feel rather than hear her laugh, which turns into a low moan as she relishes my affection.

Sam

I've closed the Night Light after the lunch rush and am wiping down tables when I hear a knock on the door.

I look up to see Luke, a loom of friendly uncertainty on his face. I unlock the door and let him in, giving him an almost awkward hug. The light brown hair that he always wore in a closely shaved cut has grown out slightly and suits him as it flicks across his brow.

"Hi stranger, how have you been?" I ask him, realising how much time has passed.

"Hi, I'm ok thanks. It's been a weird few years, I'm sure you heard about Ruby and me?" His eyes cloud over, but I just give him a sad smile.

"I know things ended and you both left, but no one ever knew the details. I'm sorry that you've been struggling" I wonder once again what happened to break them up, but decide now isn't the time to ask if he doesn't offer the information.

"Yeah, well it was a tough time. Things were over quite abruptly and all I could do was go home for some space" Is all he says, avoiding eye contact with a sigh.

"But you seem to be doing well? This place looks great!" He adds, looking around, and I try to remember what it looked like when he was last here. We haven't changed much, maybe painted a wall or two.

"Thanks, I actually really enjoy it! And you're freelance now?" I ask him, a bright smile on my face to lighten his mood.

"Yes, indeed. I moved back up North for a while, but there wasn't much work with specific companies. I ended up helping out a friend with some paperwork and decided to try some self-promoting. Its' crazy how many people are in need of accounting advice!" He laughs, and I offer him a seat.

"I'll bet! Well, funnily enough Millie may well need some advice if you'd be willing" I stay light-hearted, suddenly wary that this might be a big ask of a friend.

"Really, what's the problem?" He settles in the seat, his face serious but sympathetic.

"Do you remember a few years ago she set up her craft shop?" I pause, and he nods for me to continue, "Well, things have been tough and she needs a bit of help with figures and how to reduce costs and maximise profit I think. Does that make sense?" I look at him, hoping he'll understand.

"Of course, and I'd be happy to help. I'll give you my number and she can ring me. I'll be here for a while, and can do with all the extra work I can get to be honest. You know, being self-employed and all!" He shrugs, and writes his number down on a napkin.

"Luke thanks so much. I'll give this to her and hopefully you can stop by for a drink with us while you're here?" I feel slight trepidation and decide to take the honesty route.

"I think there's something you should know, and I'm sorry if this isn't my place or if it's not what you want to hear" I talk slowly, breaking the news of Alex and Ruby and that Alex is working here. I decide that it's the least I can do with him helping Millie; I don't want him to feel uncomfortable to come here. As I speak, I see his eyes darken, and sense that there was more to his and Ruby's split than we knew. He takes a deep breath as I finish speaking, and I can tell he's choosing his words carefully.

"Thanks Sam, I appreciate the heads up. I haven't seen Ruby since I left, and had no idea that she'd be back. I think it's best if I steer clear of her, but I'd like to meet up with you and Millie when we can" He's obviously a bit shocked, and stands up to leave. I don't stop him, but feel guilty that I've made him uncomfortable by speaking out of turn.

He gestures to the napkin he's left, and I promise to pass it on to Millie. As I fold it into the pocket of my jeans, I watch him leave and feel sad that our once close little group has been fractured beyond repair.

Millie

I've been sat in front of my laptop since Sam left me with a tube of skin cream and a smile.

She used the walk home to tell me that she'd registered me on a couple of online dating sites. I'm not sure whether to be insulted or flattered. Do I scream lonely? I've never really talked much about being single, partly because I have my business to keep me focused. I'll admit it's been a while since I actually had more than one date with the same man, but I don't have time for that kind of thing. I have stock to make and sell, to keep my pride and joy alive.

That said, I am now sat looking at the computer screen, waiting for any random man to read my profile and send me a message, or rate me, or whatever the hell people do on these things.

I can already guess that no one will stop at my picture and bother to rate it. Sam used a photo of me from her face book page, one from the Night Light that I didn't quite remember which tells you all you need to know. I've seen worse photos of myself, but it's not one that I would have chosen to show to someone who may become part of my life. Is that really what people use these sites for, or do they just scroll through the photos looking for someone they want to sleep with? I suppose I'll find out the answer if anyone actually sends me anything.

I look at my foot, at the crazy and pretty thing that I spent my day doing. I know I surprised Sam with what I did, but it's time she stopped seeing me as her innocent and cute little friend. I own my own business, and my own flat. I may not be well versed in the world of dating, but it's time she stopped looking down on me in her lovely, loving way.

Ruby

I have no idea how, but somehow I just got handed a lifeline.

I've never written a column before, but I sat in the meeting with Joe and talked through some of the gigs I've been to, adding in a few details of coursework from my Film and Media degree, and he offered me a month's trial writing for the University magazine.

I'll get paid to go to gigs around the local area, and write about them! It's not the best pay, but it should be enough to give Alex some help with the rent, and I'll actually be paid to stand and watch live music! I'm so excited, I want to get back to tell Alex, but I've promised to meet Amy in town for a coffee. Alex will be at work anyway, and I owe Amy – I've not seen her since that night that I cancelled on her. I'd feel guilty if I were able to count on one hand the amount of times that she's left me alone on a night out.

I approach the high street and see her sitting on a bench outside the coffee shop. She's talking into her mobile phone, and as I get closer I realise she's arguing with whoever's on the other end. I wave cautiously as I get closer, and she quickly ends her conversation and hangs up, a weak smile on her face.

"Hi!" She leans in to kiss me on the cheek.

"Hi, is everything it's alright?" I ask, gesturing to her phone.

"Oh, that? Yeah, it was just my mum. She wants me to come home for the weekend, but I've got things to do. Parties and stuff, you know?" She gives me a wink and a smile before marching me into the cafe.

It's a chain – Amy's choice of venue – with lots of dark wood furniture and red walls. It seems quite cosy despite the grand size, and it hasn't changed much since we used to frequent it for lazy student Sunday lunches.

We order and take a seat by a window at the back. I watch her as she checks her face in a large mirror on the wall, wanting to share my news with her but realising it's been a while since we caught up.

"So, how have you been? Things were a bit odd when you cancelled on me last week" She looks more curious than annoyed, so I decide to share all.

As I tell her about Alex and the past week, her eyes grow wide and I actually hear her gasp.

"I knew he liked you! Obviously not when he and I . . ." She wisely chooses not to finish that sentence as she sees my expression.

"Wow, so you're a real couple now?" She accepts a cappuccino from the waitress, and adds a few sugars before returning her eyes to me.

"Yeah, we are. I'm actually happy for the first time in a while" I smile, the hot chocolate that has been put in front of me filling my senses with delicious warmth.

"Well, you deserve to be babe. When we were away, it was like you had this dark cloud around you" She gives me a small apologetic look before continuing,

"You had unfinished business, you know? But now your all happy and shit" She giggles, gesturing towards my mug. I realise I've drawn a small heart in the foam and quickly sip away the evidence.

"Well, I think we need a celebration, don't you? Though, just the girls . . . I don't think Alex would agree to a night out with me anymore!" She lets out a cheeky cackle and I listen as she starts to plan our night out.

Sam

I let myself into the flat I know almost as well as my own. I can hear the noises of boys watching football in the lounge: Cheers, heckles and jeers as Ben's housemates disagree on teams.

I've come here with what men would call a one track mind, something Ben often enjoys about me. Having had my back tattoo finished, I am sore but want to show him my new ink and to keep the post-tattoo euphoria lasting as long as I can. I reach the foot of the stairs just as the half time whistle blows, and manage to catch Ben's eye as the boys start to file out in search of beer and whatever else. I wink at him and disappear up the stairs before he can so much as nod a greeting.

"Nice entrance" he says, as he closes the bedroom door behind him and raises his eyebrows in a bid to make me lower my top.

I oblige, letting the fabric drop slowly.

"Wow, its beautiful" He manages, lust darkening his eyes. He walks over to me, his fingertips floating above the skin without making contact. I feel the heat from his touch, goose bumps rising up on my back and arms in anticipation of what might happen next.

His hand finds mine and turns me round slowly, his eyes locking on mine.

"Is it sore?" He whispers.

"Slightly, but it's ok" I reply, already feeling my breath quicken as his lips brush mine. They move to my shoulder, my breast.

We move towards the armchair in the corner, where he sits down and reaches for me. His hands caress my thighs, moving under my skirt to show me how glad he is that I've interrupted his boys' night in.

Alex

I walk through to the staff room for a short break before clean up starts. I take my phone from my locker, seeing a text from Ruby I suddenly feel a smile work its way across my face.

Hey you, I got the job!! Well, a month's trial anyway. Just with Amy organising a girl's night out to celebrate. Maybe we can celebrate later when you get home?? xxxx

I check the time, less than two hours before I can be back at home with her. Even though I've not had a drink for a few weeks, the fact that Ruby has found an opportunity makes me look at my life with a stark reality check. I have a job, but it's been far from stable – admittedly, my fault – and it's not guaranteed full time. I've basically made a mess out of the last few years, and realise that I need to improve my situation if I'm to keep hold of such an amazing woman. I'm already really struggling to make ends meet and pay the rent, having not opened a few red marked letters that have fallen through the letter box.

Ironically, this means that although Ruby is making me happier than I've been for years, I'm feeling like I could happily drink to bury my head back under the sand that she dug me out from. I go to the sink and splash some water on my face, knowing I need to fight this urge; I can't fall back into the routine that could have killed me, especially now that I have everything to lose.

I send a quick but encouraging reply to Ruby, and then on the way out I glance in the mirror. The same old face stares back at me, but I relish that the vision is clear, and use that as an anchor. Somewhere inside myself, I know that I can't fuck this up again. I need to sort myself out, properly this time. As I walk back out to the bar, I hope that I can live up to the dream that I've finally started living.

Luke

I know it's stupid, but for the past few days since I saw Sam I've been in a slight haze. I probably should have guessed that Ruby and Alex would have got together after what happened. But, I can't help feeling like our relationship somehow meant less to her if she then chose him.

I'm staying in a small bed and breakfast at the end of the town, and have barely made it out of my room since the other night. I had a few meetings, which I've been to and have brought in some extra money, but the evenings have been spent watching trashy TV and drinking whisky. I'll admit that the TV was only on in the background due to the complete lack of porn available, though I'm not sure that helps my cause. I've not had a proper relationship since leaving Winchester, maybe a few nights of fun here or there, but waking up to see your girlfriend kissing another man – and evidently enjoying it – will keep you from wanting to commit again. Perhaps I was foolish for thinking a long term relationship at University would mean something, but I fell completely in love with her. I just never realised that giving her my heart would result in her smashing it into a few hundred pieces after just a few drinks.

I suddenly realise I'm staring absently at the screen as some woman in her forties is telling me how to achieve and maintain younger looking skin. I flick through some channels until Bruce Willis appears, incessantly punching someone in the face. My phone vibrates on the bedside table.

Hi Luke, it's Millie. Hope you're ok. Sam said that you might be up for giving me some help? Any chance you could pop into the shop tomorrow afternoon? I'd really appreciate your expertise, and will even buy you a few drinks afterwards. Let me know, and thanks x

I reply, knowing that I have nothing planned tomorrow, and this would give me the morning to revitalise myself to be in the best shape to help Millie. I reminisce for a second about the times before I left, spending most evenings at the Night Light listening to music and putting the world to rights with friends. I realise that Millie and Sam were always good friends, and feel guilty that I left them without a word. At least they've been welcoming upon my return, and I'll make it up to them by helping Millie to get her business back on its feet.

Ruby

I'm just succumbing to sleep as I hear the front door open. I hear Alex take off his shoes and try to pick his way quietly through to the bedroom. He sits on his side of the bed, turning on the bedside light. He looks across to see me wince, my eyes trying to adjust to the lamp.

"Shit, sorry" He says, moving to turn the light off.

"Its fine babe, you need some light to undress" I say, moving to help him take off his top. His hands catch mine and the fingers intertwine.

"You want to help?" He asks, moving my hand to his belt. He takes off his jeans and then turns towards me, his hand moving to the lamp to drown the room in darkness again.

"I wanted to wait up, but I've got to start work in the morning" I tell him, my hand caressing his cheek.

I look at the clock, which reads 02.13. I have to be up in just over five hours, and am suddenly aware of the culture shock involved in actually having a job. A lot of this job will involve going to gigs at night and then writing at home, but I still have to do a full day of training tomorrow and learn the ropes until they are satisfied that I'm competent to write the reviews at home. The last week has been idyllic; Alex's job letting us wake up lazily and make love each night without worrying about an alarm clock the next morning. I realise that this might be the first night since we got together that we've just literally slept together. Part of me feels slightly saddened, that we are reaching the part where our relationship goes from the honeymoon period to real life. I just hope that we can still make each other happy when we both have schedules and jobs to maintain.

Sam

I'd agreed to meet Millie and Luke for drinks when they'd finished working, but thought it best to meet them at the shop in case they ran late. I knock on the shop window, and wave as Luke comes to let me in.

"Already been given keys?" I ask with a smile, as he smiles a hello.

"Not quite! Millie's just going over some notes I gave her, she asked me to let you in" He ushered me into the office where Millie was leant over on the desk.

"Luke, this is brilliant. I need a few days to get through these and make some changes, but I think we're ready for the pub" Millie grins, her face turning to wink at me.

"I'm definitely ready for a drink!" Luke replies, grabbing his jacket from the back of the chair.

We walk towards the bar that Millie and I regularly drink at when I meet her from work. It recently changed management, and has had a slight overhaul but the same staff remain and the atmosphere is mostly unchanged. It has, however, become much busier since the image shift, and tonight is no different. We fight through the crowd to get to the bar, grateful when a bar man recognises us and waves us over. We order a round and find one of the few remaining tables, though I see Luke's face tighten as we walk past Ruby sat with a friend. I meet his eye with a wink, gesturing for him to start drinking as we sit down at the back of the room.

Ruby

Amy wanted to celebrate my successful first day of work in one of the nightclubs we used to frequent when we were students. I thought that might be a bit depressing, thinking back to how different things had been, and given that is was meant to indeed be a celebration.

We compromise on what had been a quaint but cool pub from my memory, but is now under new management. Amy turns her nose up as we enter, but brightens considerably when she sees the list of 'happy hour' drinks. We choose a cocktail each and then find a comfortable corner in which to devour them. It's almost an hour later that I look up from Amy's colourful story of the night I'd cancelled on her and see a face that has long since haunted my thoughts. Luke walks past with Sam and Millie – Sam seeing fit to give me a warm but concerned smile – and it's as if the last few years have vanished. I feel all the guilt, heartbreak and fear of the past slap me in the face. I take another sip of my drink and look back to Amy.

"So, basically we ended up in the back of that one guy's car. We drove for, like, an hour and then he stopped by the water and we had, like, a threesome in the car!" She laughs, and brings her cocktail stick up to her lips. There's a cherry on the end of it that she wraps round her tongue and giggles, having caught the eye of the bar man. I sigh, knowing I'll probably be left alone again tonight, when she sees my face and tuts.

"How exactly do you expect us to get free drinks if we don't flirt with the bar staff?" She asks, winking at me as she totters off to get the next round.

Alex

Having finished my shift, excited to get home and celebrate Ruby's first day, I get off the train and stop at a petrol station to get a bottle of wine and some flowers. Not the best quality, but after midnight I've learned you have to appreciate what you can find. My phone chirrups in my pocket as I'm perusing the tiny floral collection and I reach into my jeans to retrieve it. There's a missed call and voicemail from Ruby, so I manoeuvre the carrier bag into one hand to let me listen.

"Hey gorgeous, forgot to mention that Amy's chosen tonight to take me out – Might be home before you if she deserts me again . . . I love you"

My disappointment is quickly outshone by the last few words, which make my heartbeat seem to catch in my throat. Ruby's never said she loved me before, and I wish that she was walking with me so I could see her face. After that embarrassingly honest speech that I gave her when we got together, I'd been waiting in hope of this moment and I feel strong and shaky all at the same time.

I check the time of the text, and realise it was sent less than an hour ago. I sigh, looking at the flowers and wondering whether to reply, or whether Ruby will be too drunk by now to read it. I like Amy, evidently I liked her too much once, but I remember her being able to handle as much alcohol as I can.

I buy a small bunch of flowers to leave in a vase – I'm sure Kate must have left one somewhere – but choose vodka over wine and resign myself to a night on my own. Why this saddens me so much, I'm not sure. I'd just got so used to being happy with Ruby that I've not really thought of what to do with myself when I'm alone. I plan to relax on the sofa with a small glass of vodka and watch some action film that Ruby would be bored by. The wind blows the hair into my face as I walk towards the flat; I shake my head and drag my hand through my fringe, hoping that Amy won't lead my girlfriend astray.

Luke

I've been sat with Sam and Millie for a few hours now, getting slowly but extremely drunk. I can't remember the last time I had such a good time with friends, but all I wish is that I could stop looking into the mirror by the bar and watching Ruby. She's still the most gorgeous girl I've ever seen, and it will always break my heart to know that I wasn't enough to keep her happy.

She was always close to Alex, but in my complete love for her I didn't see what was happening. They must have laughed about it, while they got drunk together and realised how much better they were for each other. She begged me to understand that nothing had happened before that night, but she must have thought I was a fool to believe it. I'll admit, I'm ashamed to remember raising my hand to her, but I had a mental block. I opened the door, thinking Ruby had fallen asleep on the sofa, and saw the love of my life kissing my best friend. My best friend that I realised later must have been in love with her for a long time. The look on his face as he left our home isn't something that you can fake.

I felt this odd feeling of rage and frustration and – pathetically – jealousy come over me. I saw in Ruby's eyes a passion that I hadn't seen for a while, and I didn't even notice until afterwards.

When I woke up the next morning, I knew that I had to leave; we wouldn't have been able to get past that night. She'd always said that she'd never tolerate violence in a relationship, shame I never got the chance to tell her that I felt the same about infidelity. She never asked, so I had to show her.

2010: (3 Years Later)
Ruby

My head hurts.

Not even in the hung-over, fun way that it used to. I remember those nights; when Alex and I would go to the pub for hours and wile away the time with our friends. Even when we were together, we'd spend evenings drinking wine and listening to music or going to gigs. I always loved that we shared our passion for live music, but now things are a bit different.

Now my head hurts because I've not slept for almost 30 hours. My beautiful - but mischievous – little girl is recovering from an ear infection and hasn't let me sleep.

I open my eyes as I hear Mae begin to whimper. She sees my face and whines until I drag myself up to sit and reach across the bed for her. I don't usually let Mae sleep in our bed, but when she's ill it's the only way that my baby will drift off. I cradle her in my arms, and can see from her smile that she's on the mend.

I should ring Alex and reassure him that we're fine. He was worried and reluctant to go into work this morning, but I was hopeful that she just needed some rest. It's been a tough few months for Alex; He's worked his ass off for a few years and finally Sam suggested him to take over her managerial position at the Night Light. She has been mentoring him for a while, giving him extra responsibility during the times that she was away in Bristol with Ben. He's been offered a job there – some kind of sports massage therapist – and asked her to move with him. Basically it's meant that Alex has been working lots of overtime to prove that he's up to the job of managing the bar, which can be a bit of a struggle with a two-year-old to manage.

Luckily, I've been able to cut my work down to part time freelance articles. I love music journalism, but it's a slightly impractical profession for a new mother. My work currently consists of reviewing performances that are family friendly along with a few weekly columns that I write for some local magazines. The money isn't great, but with Alex's salary set to rise we should be OK for the time being. Alex's parents send care packages regularly to help out, and my mum comes to visit whenever she can – thankfully – and we love our little bundle of joy. Things are good, even more so now that Mae is giggling in my ear and asking for chocolate buttons.

Alex always says she looks more like me, but I think she has his eyes. Her hair is a mixture of the two – The colour of chocolate (like mine) but in the last year we've let it grow and it's developed that gorgeous, tousled texture that Alex's has. She likes to play with it, just like I do, and always tends to try and eat it when she's sleepy. Alex has become a fan of dressing her like a 'celebrity child' as he calls it, letting Mae pick out a mixture of absurd patterns to team together in strange ensembles.

Today though, we're having a pyjama day to let her rest and recover, so she's dressed in a cute little pink and yellow sleep suit that Alex's mum sent over last week. She's trying to steal the covers from me to use as a cape, which is annoying when Alex tries it, but somehow you can't be angry with a two-year-old when they're poorly.

Alex

I check my phone again, hoping that no news is good news.

Mae looked so sad when I left this morning, her little hands reaching out to me as I got ready for work. Ruby wouldn't let me stay, knowing how important it is for me to make a good impression now that I'm finally being given the chance to step up. Sam sees my face as I slide my phone back into my pocket.

"Is everything alright at home?" She asks, her face betraying the concern of a close friend.

"I hope so, Mae wasn't well last night. I asked Ruby to ring, but nothing yet" I shrug, hoping to show my professionalism above parental worry.

"I'm sure she'll be fine, no news is good news" Sam states, voicing my hope with a quick smile.

We go through the cashing up procedure again, and I add to my notes from the last few times. It all seems straightforward, but I spent a long time disappointing Sam when I started working here so I want to get everything right and show her that I'm worthy of her time.

"Has Ben gone back to Bristol?" I ask, knowing that his job was to do with the University. Given that it's September, and that Sam is slightly distracted too, I'm guessing that term time may have started.

"Yeah, he left a few days ago. I'll be meeting him there next week, once you're up to speed and I've spent some time with Millie" She frowns, and I see how hard it will be for her to leave her best friend.

"You'll still come back to see us though, yeah?" I ask, offering her a smile.

"Of course, but it's not quite the same" She sighs, then gathers herself, asking me to go through my notes again while she hides her face and goes to make us some coffee.

Millie

I seem to have finished almost a full bottle of wine.

I'm not quite sure how I did it, or how I'll explain it to Sam. It was her bottle, after all.

I got back from my second date with Max, a man that Ben shared a flat with after finishing his course, and somehow decided to open my laptop and start looking on the dating sites that I have now become proficient in. It was quite obvious that Max was more interested in the waitress than me, so I wondered if any of the websites that Sam had made me register with would bring any joy.

Quite the opposite.

A few men had sent me messages, but it was evident from their photos – and the messages – that they weren't looking for more than a one-night stand. I'm not surprised, nor am I of the mindset that that's the wrong way to go about internet dating. It's something I quite enjoyed a few times during the early days after Sam set up my profiles.

After a few months, though, I realised that I wasn't really cut out for casual sex. It was fun, but it wasn't what I wanted. I wanted what Sam and Ben had: I wanted a boyfriend. I'd had boyfriends before, but never long term relationships. I had grown to envy the friends who seemed to fall easily in love. Maybe one day that would be me, but for now I had to appease myself with a bottle of wine and photos of men who had 'rated' or 'slated' an image that showed a confident and slightly drunk version of a girl that I no longer wanted to be.

Sam

It's been over a week now since Ben left for Bristol, and I miss him. I never thought I'd get so deep into a relationship that I'd struggle to cope by myself.

We've been together for almost five years now – by far the longest time for both of us – and I can't help wondering whether this move to Bristol will bring everything into place. I'm so sad to be leaving Millie, but this job could be great for Ben and I'm not sure either of us could be happy dealing with a long distance thing. She's reassured me that she understands, but I've noticed her distancing herself for the last few weeks and it worries me.

After leaving Alex to lock up at the bar, I walk towards home and glance at the time on my phone. Realising it's almost 10pm I rub my neck and ring Ben.

"Hey, how's your day been?" He greets me, though I can hear distraction in his voice.

"Hey, it's been long. Alex is learning well though. How are things with you?" I ask, my thighs arguing as I start to climb the hill at the top of the high street.

"Good, a few of us have gone for a drink to celebrate the end of the first week of training. It's getting a bit messy, but I'll be good I promise" He chuckles, and I hear people shouting in the background.

"Sounds like your busy babe. Have a good night and ring me tomorrow? Love you" I reply, wishing I could be there with him.

"You too" He says, and hangs up.

It's only as I put away my phone that I register what he'd said, and wonder why he'd felt the need to promise to behave.

Ben

I turn over as I hear my alarm, and wince slightly as my head disagrees with the movement.

As I hung up from speaking to Sam last night, I had every intention of going home. A few of the other teachers had different ideas, though. Bristol's faculty seems to have more than its fair share of dance teachers: A few muscular male choreographers, but mainly newly trained women. I love Sam, but being far away from her with this much temptation is tough. I'm trying to be what she deserves, and I will keep trying, but having a group of single, limber young dancer types vying for your affection is making me doubt myself.

I get up, wishing that I'd been strong enough to turn down the shots of tequila at closing time, and make myself some strong coffee. My phone beeps with a message, and I pick it up from the tiny dining table. As I glance at the screen I see there are two new texts.

Morning babe, hope you're not too delicate this morning? I can't wait to meet all your new friends. Miss you, Sam xx

Hey lightweight, how's the head? We'll have to do it again before term starts ;) Xx

I realise with concern that the second text could have been from any of the three dance teachers, as there is a number but no name attached. I remember most names from the week's training and so 1 scroll through my contacts and conclude that there's only one whose number I don't have saved. I then try, unsuccessfully, to remember the name of the girl who isn't in my phone.

Given the nameless girl, and the tone of the text, I decide that it's best to only reply to the message sent by my actual girlfriend.

Alex

By the time I get home from work, Ruby and Mae are fast asleep on the bed. I'd put up a fight last night when Ruby had brought Mae into our bed, but she was so exhausted that I didn't feel I could win the argument so I relented. I look at them now, the two ladies in my heart, and all I want to do is join them so we can fall asleep in a pretty tableau.

As I move to sit down and take off my trainers, Ruby stirs and turns. I watch her face and stand up, not wanting to disturb her or my beautiful child. Instead I walk through to the lounge and sit down on the small sofa, opening the bottom drawer of the nearby cabinet as I do so. The cabinet is small, and has always housed my paperwork. The bottom drawer, though, just has a few receipts. The receipts have recently been able to hide the small black box that I sometimes take out at times like this when I'm alone and want to remember how lucky I am.

A few years ago I was in a bad way, and Ruby saved me from a downward spiral that I don't like to think about. We got together, and then we quickly became a little family. It was a surprise, but one that I wouldn't take back. Mae has given us a reason to fight for this relationship whenever things get rough, and she has seemed to reinforce the love that I've had for Ruby for years.

Ruby and I talked about marriage before we were together, and neither of us thought it to be necessary. I'm not sure whether she still feels that way, but I'm hoping that having Mae has made Ruby as ready as I am to make this family official. I'm a bit scared to start the conversation, knowing that she was never the kind of girl who dreamt about weddings, but I think I know her well enough now that she'll trust I can make her and Mae happy for the rest of our lives.

I look up at the clock on the wall and realise I've been sat thinking for almost an hour. I replace the box in its drawer, and make my way back into the bedroom. I don't want to wake them, but I can't keep myself from sleep anymore and I don't want to belong anywhere else, so I undress silently and fold myself into the small space left beside my girls.

Sam

I've been packing all afternoon, since Alex sent me home this morning. He assured me that he was comfortable with the management stuff, gave me a hug and sent me off to pastures new with my boyfriend. I admit now that Ruby has been really good for him; he never would have stepped up like this if she hadn't come back to him.

Millie always closes the shop on a Sunday, so she's been at home with me. She's fluttered between helping me pack, crying and offering me wine so she's not drinking alone. I feel really sad to be leaving her alone here, though she'll have Alex, Ruby and Mae to keep her busy. The shop is doing well, and she's been on a few dates recently so I think she's just around the corner from a good relationship. When I tell her this over our second glass of wine, however, she snorts until the wine gets stuck in her nose.

"I'm not sure, Sam. Do you remember that guy Max that Ben set me up with? Five hours after our date, he commented on Face book about the great sex he'd had with that waitress!" She laughs, though I can see in her eyes that she was hurt by this.

"OK, so we can forget him. Have you looked on the dating sites for any more men?" I ask, abandoning my suitcase to join her on the bed and open the laptop.

"I've given up on them; perhaps I'll just become a lesbian. Want to join me?" She leans across and gives me a peck on the lips, until we both collapse in laughter.

"Seriously Mills, I feel awful leaving you here. Are you sure you'll be OK?" I ask, looking into the eyes of the only best friend I've ever had.

"Sam, I'll be fine. I've got my own business, and I've promised some extra childcare to Ruby to keep me busy. It's not like I need money for the mortgage, go and have your own life with Ben" She says, making me feel slightly guilty for having lived here rent free due to her Nan's inheritance.

"So, I should finish packing and then we can finish the wine? I've told Ben I'll be there by tomorrow lunch time" I've not even finished the sentence before Millie reaches over to fill up my glass.

Ben

I really need to stop drinking now.

I'd spent three years getting drunk between sports lectures, and thought the friends from my course were fairly hardcore when it came to nights out. It seems I was misinformed: No one can get drunk like a group of young dance teachers.

We'd started as a full faculty group, enjoying the last night of letting our hair down before term starts next week. We have fresher's week first so the course timetable doesn't begin for a week, and with Sam arriving tomorrow I wanted to have a last group night out before I spend time with her. Most people had left early, leaving me and the English lecturer along with the three dance teachers. Matt, the English guy, is nice enough but is in his forties and the girls are trying to get me to agree to leave him stranded so we can go to the next bar along the waterfront and dance the night away. I don't want to make any enemies, but after a few rounds of tequila, I fear I'm being easily led.

I'm also struggling to remember all the girl's names. I know one of them is Sophie, as she stuck in my head as the one who was willing to demonstrate the splits in the first bar we'd drank in tonight. I love Sam, but for some reason I can't fight a certain image that Sophie put into my head with that display. I'm almost certain that Sophie is the girl who's not in my phone, so I feel no need to remember the others. Instead, I accept the shot glass put in front of me, and then when it's empty I decide it's for the best to follow the girls as they grab my hand and run for the door. I can't see Matt, but he can't be far behind.

Millie

For some reason, I'm unable to sleep again.

It may be because I know that Sam will be gone this time tomorrow, and I feel like I'll be stuck here on my own after she leaves. I can't tell her any of this though, she's my best friend and I want her to be happy.

We fell asleep on the sofa after too much wine and, predictably, watching Bridget Jones' Diary. Sam had tried to coerce me into one of her indie films, but I wanted the comfort and stability that this film brought.

I get up, careful not to wake her, and pull a blanket from the back of the sofa to keep her warm. I walk into the kitchen, pouring and drinking a large glass of water, before pausing in the doorway, watching my best friend sleep. Her phone beeps, making me jump and almost spill my drink. I take the phone from the table, checking in case it's important. As I glance at the screen, I feel myself freeze on the spot.

Hey Sarah, where are you?? Lost you and my phone, but Ben lives near so crashing there tonight ;) Tell all tmrw, Soph xx

What the hell is that about?

I panic, wishing I'd never picked up the phone. Who's Sarah, who's Soph? More importantly, why is some random girl staying in Ben's flat and sending texts to Sam?!

I'm in two minds whether to wake her, but I know what she'd want me to do. I take a deep breath and stroke her shoulder, not quite sure what I should say when she wakes up.

Sam

I can't remember ever being this angry.

I had no idea what to do when Millie woke me late last night, but I knew I had to do something. I decided - after a teary conversation with Millie – to wake up early this morning and get to Bristol before Ben would expect me. If there really was a random girl in his flat, he'd have explaining to do. I was hoping it was all a misunderstanding, Ben would never be unfaithful, but I needed him to prove it after that message.

The roads are clear, and I arrive before 10am. I let myself into the flat and walk quietly through the living room, my eyes looking for anything out of place. I catch my face in the hallway mirror and frown. There could easily be a reason for this, I think suddenly. I need to trust Ben and look towards our life together. I'm suddenly unsure of what I'm doing, until I realise that I'm just here a few hours early and he was expecting me today.

I open the bedroom door, part of me ready to undress and get into bed to wake him slowly and sexily. I stop as I see he's not alone. There's a girl next to him in bed, our bed. I feel nauseous as I realise that the sheets aren't quite covering everything, and I can see that both her and my boyfriend are naked.

I feel myself shaking, so much so that I

stumble and grab the door for support. The door knocks against the wall, making a loud noise in the silence of the flat. I see Ben stir, turning onto his back and draping an arm across the girl's body. His hand settles on her breast in a sleepy gesture that I'd come to know and enjoy. Seeing him touch her makes me breathless, and I begin to cough quietly. I realise that I need to get out, just as his eyes open and lock on mine. I almost see his brain try to work through the hangover and process what he's woken up to. I want to stay and see what he does, but I know that I may faint if I don't get fresh air and try to block out the scene I've been faced with.

I run as fast as my legs will carry me, locking the front door in case he tries to follow me out, and manage to find and select Millie's number with one hand. Impressive, really, under the circumstances.

Ben

What the hell just happened?

The last thing I remember is doing a shot of tequila – albeit not the first – and following the girls out of a bar. I have no idea how I went from there to here.

My head is throbbing, and I'm in serious danger of throwing up, but I seem to be naked in bed with someone that isn't Sam.

This is bad, really bad. I have no idea what's happened, but I think I may have just seen Sam flee from my room. So, this is somewhere really far past the point of bad.

I look around and locate my jeans, seeing a black lacy thong with the word 'Juicy' stitched in pink on the front. I feel a wave of guilt and revulsion wash over me. I run through the flat, confused when I find the front door locked. Did I really see Sam, or was it a dream? Walking back through to the kitchen, the clock reads 9.52. It's surely too early for Sam, but I definitely need lots of water, and to get the naked girl out of my bed.

I sit on the sofa with the glass of water and try to clear my head. I've obviously completely fucked up, but the clouds behind my eyes seem to be leading me to other thoughts. I close them and see Sam's face, filled with horror, staring down at me as I wake up. Was she really here?

I look around, searching for an answer. The lounge looks the same as I left, in need of a tidy but with only my belongings in it. I walk over to the front door, noticing that the key isn't in the lock where it usually lives at night. It's been strewn across the floor, something that happens if the door is unlocked from the outside. I try to open the door, but it's locked so I have to retrieve the key from the floor to get out. So, Sam has definitely been here this morning, and then she locked herself back out.

I half sigh, half laugh at my own stupidity as I open the door. Looking out onto the street, I see Sam's car parked across the road. Glad that I at least remembered to put on jeans as I left the bedroom, I walk tentatively towards her little black Mini Cooper. Before I reach it though, the engine starts up and she speeds away. I step back to stop her hitting me, and she locks eyes with me again. I don't remember ever seeing such contempt, anger, hatred and heartbreak all in one expression. I stumble on the kerb and somehow find myself sitting in the street, calling her name and wondering how the hell I could be such an idiot.

Ruby

I get up from my desk, abandoning my article in frustration, and walk over to the CD player.

Alex has taken Mae to the park for a few hours so that I can catch up with my weekly columns. The deadline is almost upon me for a gig review article I write bi-weekly. I was including write-ups of a festival that I'd been to over the summer, and had been alternating some indie albums to inspire the review's completion, but I was struggling to clear my head.

I feel the need for an album to soothe and feed my brain, given that I've not really managed a full night's sleep in the last week. I flick through a pile of albums that are yet to be filed in the shelves. A few are EPs that I've collected from support acts, but I feel the need for a comforting, familiar sound. I pick up Ellie Goulding's CD, though it's more upbeat than I want today. I put it down and pause on Imogen Heap, before my eyes fall on a CD that I bought only last week.

Alex and I had been to a tiny gig in Southampton as our first 'date night' since Mae was born. My mum had come to stay and had looked after her granddaughter for a few hours. It was a band called Stornoway and, as we've often done for my reviews, we went to the gig on the strength of one single. I loved them, and rushed straight out to buy the album when it came out. They were perhaps too folky to be main stream, but the album has been frequently in the CD player since and has even helped us to get Mae to sleep.

As the first song begins, I sit down on the sofa, leaning back into the cushions and letting my body relax for a moment. I feel my breath deepen and let the music take me away to a calm and quiet place.

Alex

Mae looks up at me with those beautiful eyes that she shares with Ruby, and she asks if we can go home.

I smile, knowing that she wants to see her mum. Mae is always keen to be with Ruby when she's under the weather. We'd thought that some fresh air would help her get rid of the last of the infection, but she's been quiet since we left home. She looks tired, so I secure her in the push chair and manoeuvre towards the path.

I almost collide with a small group of men as we get back towards the pavement: They are carrying beer cans and are clearly a bit worse for wear. One of them heckles me as I sigh and push past them onto the street. Looking at my watch, I see that it's almost 3pm. I remember the days of being drunken students, but the men look more my age. I take a quick glance behind me, relieved that they've moved on and won't hassle me and Mae.

I never pictured myself having a family in my twenties, and with Kate the idea of settling down seemed so alien and out of the question. Somehow with Ruby, even though Mae wasn't planned, I was thrilled at the idea of making a family together. It was a relief to realise that perhaps Kate was just not the person I was meant to spend my life with, and being so comfortable with fatherhood – though it took Ruby a little while to agree – makes me so grateful that things happened how they did. I feel like I belong with my two beautiful girls much more than I would belong with a slightly pathetic, drunken group of men terrorising the local park of an afternoon.

We finally arrive at our front door, and with a glance I see that Mae has fallen into a much needed sleep. I bring the pushchair into the lounge and leave my sleeping baby in the corner, as I see Ruby, also asleep, on the sofa. She stirs as I sit down beside her, and the smile she offers makes me kiss her softly but deeply.

"Hi" She says, pleased with my sudden affection.

"Hey, did you finish your article?" I ask, looking over to her laptop.

"Almost, but I sat down for a break and must have fallen asleep. How was the park?" She yawns, rubbing the sleep from her eyes.

"It was fun, but Mae was tired and wanted you" I laugh, as Ruby smiles.

"She seems nearly better, but we're both tired from the last few days I think" I see Ruby look up at the laptop and I have an idea.

"I know babe, but how about this? I'm not working tonight, so I'll take care of Mae while you finish your work and have a proper sleep. Then if she's better tomorrow, we can ask Millie to watch her and I can take you out for dinner?" I think of the little box in the drawer and smile as Ruby's mouth touches mine.

"I love you, you know that?" She says, as I laugh at her and suddenly feel excitement and nerves dance together in my stomach.

Kate

I can't believe it.

A few years ago, the idea of parenthood scared the shit out of Alex, so much so that he ended a seven-year relationship and expected me to move on while he screwed his best friend.

I knew that he was falling in love with her, long before he admitted it, but he still felt the need to mess me around and break my heart into the bargain. I left in a daze, wanting nothing more to do with him. I could barely look him in the eye: My little white lie suddenly outweighed by the fact that our time together had dwindled to nothing in his head. I ran home, leaving him to the flat because I quite honestly couldn't deal with the communication. I felt humiliated, rejected and like I needed time with my family to lick my wounds and mend my heart, which had just been smashed to pieces without so much as a thought.

I drove back to Ipswich, decided to sever all ties and be at home for a while until I felt more like me again. I buried myself in teaching - landing a nice job quite quickly in a nearby primary school - and spent some time with my niece to ease my broodiness.

I didn't let myself think about Alex, other than during the nights when my sister, Ali, insisted on sharing a bottle of wine and playing my therapist.

I've not fully dealt with things enough to get over him, and haven't so much as been on a date since I moved back to Ipswich. I'd not let any of it impact on me enough to hurt, until an old friend from my course emailed me with an invitation to a teacher's reunion. The idea of seeing some old friends was lovely, but it took a long time for them – and Ali – to convince me to go. Ali said that if I didn't go back and get some closure, maybe finding Alex alone and drunk in a gutter, that I'd never let myself have a relationship again. I'd always wanted a family, so I knew that I had some demons to confront before I could finally move on.

I'd travelled down the night before the reunion to give myself a bit of time to settle and find my bearings again. The reunion was in Winchester, but I knew Southampton much better so I booked a B and B there and would just drive the short distance tomorrow. Once I'd checked into my room, I went for a walk and found myself being pulled back to our flat. I'd half expected to see someone else living there, but as I round the corner I see the ex-love of my life manoeuvring up to the door with a pushchair. From the way he handles it, and the baby, it's obvious that he's not babysitting. His face is the picture of paternal love, even from this distance.

I seek cover, hiding in an alleyway until I hear the front door close. I wonder who the mother is, hoping to hell that it's not Ruby. I think I'd go crazy if she'd not only got her hands on my boyfriend, but had the family that I wanted.

I wipe my face, realising that I'm crying, and dejectedly walk back to the B and B. I stop at our old local off licence on the way – I've never been a keen drinker, but I suddenly need something strong to numb myself.

Sam

I find it really hard to focus on driving, so I pull over and find my phone. There are seven missed calls from Ben, which I'm never likely to return, and a text message from Millie.

Hey, what happened? Worried about you babe, ring me xx

I dial her number, realising that it rang out when I left Ben's and I didn't leave a message. I fill her in as best as I can between sobs, admitting that I've parked up and am a complete mess. Millie, amazing friend that she is, orders me to sit tight and wait for her. I'm parked quite close to the train station, so she's coming to meet me. I promise to pay her back as soon as I can.

It'll take her a few hours, so she rings when she's boarded the train and then tells me to go for a walk to clear my head and not to answer my phone unless it's her. By now, I have almost twenty missed calls and a few messages from Ben, but I delete them all without checking them and lock up my car ready for some fresh air. I don't know Bristol well, but I'd been driving for almost half an hour when I stopped so there's little chance of him finding me.

Ben

Sam's voicemail kicks in again, and I toss my phone aside. It lands with a thud on the concrete, all at once reminding me that I have a horrific hangover and that I'm still sat on the pavement.

I get up, ignoring my screaming head but retrieving my phone, and can almost feel my tail dragging between my denim clad legs as I shut the door behind me. I look into my text messages, trying to remember what I've sent to Sam. A strange message catches my eye as I scrawl through the list and I feel anger and nausea in equal measure.

After relieving my stomach, I march through to the bedroom where the naked girl – Sophie I now realise after seeing the text – is still lying asleep on my bed. The bed that Sam and I bought together for the life I've just completely screwed up, with a lot of help from the slut I spent last night with. I reach across and pull the covers off her, having a sudden need to wake her without touching her very naked body. She turns over, her eyes opening slightly. They alight on me and a cheeky smile crosses her lips.

"Hey babe, are you coming back to bed?" She sees my expression and her smile disappears.

"Did you text my girlfriend last night?" I ask, working hard to keep my voice even.

"What?" I can see her brain trying to work things out, and then she winces.

"I lost my phone! I text Sarah so she'd know I was safe" She looks at me with a pained expression, though whether it was shame or hangover I couldn't tell.

"Yeah, well, it seems you were as wasted as I was. You sent that text to my girlfriend. Who, it turns out, came by this morning and now won't answer my calls. You need to get your stuff and leave" I lean across and pull her out of bed. I find a few of her clothes on the floor and throw them in her direction.

"Dude, I'm so sorry!" She actually has the gall to giggle.

"Seriously? This is funny to you?!" My anger seems stronger than my hangover and I pick up her bag and bra, hung so elegantly over my bedpost.

"Hey, I didn't force you to sleep with me. You obviously don't love her if you wanted me after – "I don't even hear the rest of the sentence as I march her out of the flat, throwing her bag and jacket into the street after her.

I sit back down on the sofa, aware of the hypocrisy that I just gave into. I can't blame some random girl for what I did last night. They fed me tequila, but no one held a gun to my head. I don't know what to do, I can't quite think clearly past the shame, guilt and anger. The anger is directed at me for being so weak as to get drunk and sleep with some dance teacher purely because I miss my girlfriend.

I look back at my phone, knowing that there will be no messages from Sam. I have no idea what to do, but I know I may have just lost the first person I ever truly loved.

Millie

I'm not sure I can describe how angry I feel.

I've been on a train for just over an hour, trying to work out what to say to my best friend whose boyfriend – EX boyfriend – decided to go out and sleep with someone else the night before they were planning to start a new life together in a town completely new and foreign to my friend.

Sam had been so unsure of moving away, having spent so long building a life in Winchester. I'd spent many nights discussing it with her, letting her bounce ideas and fears off me and not daring to ask her to stay. We thought she'd finally found someone who would make her happy and she'd looked into bar work in Bristol and even set up a meeting with a restaurant on the waterfront, excited at the prospect of getting involved with the food side of things.

Now, Sam's new life has been ripped away before it started. I now know that I did the right thing in waking her last night – I never thought that anything untoward had actually happened. I trusted Ben but I had to make sure he was worthy of that trust. It turns out that he's just like all the rest of the bastards that I've met on the internet dating sites: He can't quite give up the thrill of the chase for love.

I check my phone, seeing that there's only

half an hour left of my journey. I ring Sam to let her know that all's going to plan and I'll be in Bristol soon. She's been walking and feels slightly less like a confused zombie, though it will probably be some time before she feels human and happy again. Luckily I'm on her cars' insurance and can rescue her and take her home.

Kate

I reach for the coffee mug and smile politely at the B and B owner.

I drank half a bottle of red wine last night, only absorbed by a small pot of tomato pasta that I found looking lonely on the fridge shelf of the off licence. I feel awful today. Alex used to try and make me share bottles of wine with him when I lived in that flat. I never liked the taste, though I've no doubt that Ruby drank her share and loved it.

I hid the wine bottle in my bag, not wanting Mrs. Sutton – the owner – to know I'd been drinking alone instead of out dancing all night with friends as I'm sure most of her lodgers do. I'm sure that she and her husband saw me scuttle back to my room before 7pm with my sad little pasta and wine, but surely there's no need to speak of it. Instead I swallow the much needed caffeine and ignore the troubled smile that she gives me.

Today I had planned to drive into Winchester and wander around, in the hope that Alex and Ruby will be a safe train ride away. I'm not meeting the other teachers until 6.30pm for a meal at Pizza Express before the reunion a few hours later. It wasn't my choice of restaurant, as it always brings to mind Alex trying to coerce me out with his friends when we were students. At least I have plenty of time to drink water and rid myself of this god awful headache before tonight.

I thank Mrs. Sutton for the coffee, insisting that I'll get a full breakfast in town. I pick up my bag and walk through the gate into car park. After the short drive, and the fluke of finding a cheap, long stay parking spot, it strikes me that I've never really spent time in the centre of Winchester before: The train station is the opposite direction, and I've never taken the time to explore the bottom end of the high street. I decide to look for the restaurant first so I can get my bearings for later, then I'll find somewhere that serves fry ups – A meal I've not ordered for years, but am in dire need of today.

Alex

I step out of the shower and dry myself off.

I rang Millie this morning to ask for babysitting support tonight. She was unsure, mentioning something about a trip to Bristol, but then when I admitted my plan for the evening, she got excited and said that she and Sam would be back and glad to help. I had thought that Sam had already left for Bristol but wasn't going to ask questions when two of Mae's favourite people were around to watch Disney films and play with her for a few hours.

As I walk through to the bedroom, Ruby is getting out of bed. I pull her towards me as I hear Mae start to gurgle in the crib.

"Millie and Sam are up for babysitting tonight. Do you think Mae's well enough?" I ask, my eyes looking hopefully into Ruby's.

"She was fine last night, but I'll make sure she has a nap this afternoon. Where do you want to go for dinner?" She smiles, her fingers enveloping mine.

"Thought you might want to go into Winchester for an Italian? It was your favourite back in the student days" Her smile lingers and becomes a grin, telling me that I've read her mind.

"Sounds wonderful babe, I can't wait" She kisses me lightly and walks over to entertain our baby.

Sam

So, my life is officially a complete mess.

I walked for an hour and then somehow found my way back to my car. I've been sat inside for a while now and just can't fathom any thoughts beyond that.

I gave up everything for Ben: My job, which I loved, and my home with Millie. OK, so that might still be available, but the job has been given to Alex, who deserves it.

I sacrificed everything for a man that I loved. I shared my life with him for four years, and the night before our new life started, he decided to have sex with someone that he'd just met. When I first met him, he admitted to having slept with a lot of girls. I was quite relieved by that, having had more than my fair share of one night stands. I have never, however, been unfaithful. I admit that Ben was my first long term relationship, but his longest relationship before us was only a few months, so we were on equal ground. I had happily left behind my past for something more. It turns out that Ben hadn't, so both of us were screwed but in different ways.

My phone starts to chirp and I realise I've been sat in a daze for a long time.

Millie is ringing me.

As I answer the call, my car shakes. I jump,

looking to the figure knocking at the window. It's Millie.

I open the passenger door, and let her climb in and hold me as a fresh wave of tears seep out onto my skin.

"What the hell happened?!" She asks, cuddling me as I sob.

It takes a while before my breath is steady enough to recount my morning to her. Somehow, telling the story to the person I trust most in the world seems to stop my tears.

"What a bastard!" She says, making me laugh and cry at the same time.

She orders me to climb into the back seat and covers me with a blanket. She then pulls the sat nav from the glove box where it sleeps, sets our flat as the destination and tells me to lie down and try to sleep.

"Rest now babe, I'll take us home. Oh, and I promised Alex that we'd babysit Mae tonight. We can watch Disney films and have cuddles. Get some sleep" With that, she indicates and turns onto the main road. I'm not sure what to say, so I close my eyes and try to forget the day so I can start again when I wake.

<u>*Ruby*</u>

Alex has gone into work for a few hours to make sure that the staff can handle two days without him.

I don't really understand the logic in this, but I'm enjoying the time with Mae. Now that she's better, she's all smiles and has gone down for her nap without a fight.

I need to finish my articles before the end of the week, so I'm sat in front of my laptop again. I'm still struggling to get the words out, and can't figure out why. I decide to look for some of my older articles to read through in search of inspiration.

I can't remember where I put my folder with all my past articles, so I start to hunt through the drawers next to the desk. I can't find it, finally opening the bottom drawer that's stuffed with receipts and some of Alex's old stuff.

I resolve to tell him he needs to clear out his crap, but as I try to close the drawer I see a box lying under the papers. My heart rate quickens as I reach for it, sensing that I'm not meant to see the contents. Do I open it? I shouldn't, but somehow I can't put it down.

Suddenly, the front door opens and Alex strides through. I drop the box, but don't have time to close the drawer before he sees me.

"Hey, thought you'd be working for longer?" I say, trying to bide some time but it seems I've been caught.

"They were doing fine, sent me home in fact" He smiles, his expression not faltering as he sees me.

"Oh, I meant to tell you I bought that. Did you open it? It's for my mum's birthday present" He walks past me and picks up the box. He opens it and I see a lovely silver bracelet with charms hanging from it. One has a picture of Mae, and the others are small, pretty gemstones.

"Alex, she'll love it" I say, almost breathless.

"Thanks, I forgot I left it there" He kisses my forehead, taking the box and walking into the bedroom.

I sit back, my hand moving to my heart where I can still feel a quickened beat. As it slows to its normal rate, I can't tell whether I feel proud that Alex was so thoughtful with his mum, or disappointed that the gift wasn't what I'd thought.

Ben

OK, so I've been sat on the sofa for perhaps a few hours. I've been staring at my phone, willing Sam to ring or text me.

I know it will probably never happen, but I've got to do something to win her back. I have no idea what that could be, and my hangover keeps getting in the way of my pathetic brainstorming.

I can't let this be the end of us, not after so many years. Sam's the only person that I've ever loved and I won't lose that over a stupid, drunken mistake with a woman who wears knickers with 'juicy' written on them.

Perhaps if I go to see her: I know she'll have gone back to Millie's and will probably be almost there by now. Millie, though I'm fond of her, will be telling Sam to forget about me and probably men in general. They'll be planning to spend time together to heal the pain while Sam still – hopefully – keeps thinking about what a great life we could be living together. Apart from the fact that I stamped on her heart until I crushed it . . . .

So, my plan needs some more brain storming, but I will sit here until I come up with a fool proof way to win her back.

Alex

Ruby has finally finished her articles, and is having a shower before getting ready for our dinner date.

I'm stood in the bedroom, trying to decide which shirt to wear. Girls never understand this: They think that choosing outfits is a purely female problem. Ruby, luckily, has had years of helping me choose the right shirt, and the fact that she understands my idiosyncrasies still makes me smile.

I walk across to my bedside table, listening out to make sure that the shower is still running. I open my top drawer and reach right to the back, checking for the familiar little black box. I'd had to move it from the lounge when I realised Ruby was struggling to finish her work. She's done that before and ends up upending any and all storage boxes to find old articles. Luckily, my mum's birthday is coming up and it was a genius way (if I say so myself) to gauge what Ruby's reaction would be. The look of shock on her face last night when I caught her and disappointment when she found mum's present gave me a small jolt of excitement and happiness.

I replace the box as I hear the shower finish, not wanting her to know anything until the moment after dinner when I ask her to be my wife.

I pick the green shirt that I know she loves, and am almost dressed when she comes into the room.

"Wow, looking gorgeous darling" She smiles at me, her hand caressing my chest.

"Thanks babe. You too" I grin, kissing her long and deep while she's still dressed in only a towel. She pulls away, slightly flushed and smiling.

"When are Sam and Millie due?" She asks, perusing her own wardrobe.

"In the next half an hour, but I can sort them out while you get ready" I kiss her lightly on her bare shoulder as I make my way through to Mae in the lounge, currently being happily amused by Peppa Pig.

Kate

I'm sat in a strange pub, looking at my sad reflection in a cracked mirror on the wall.

The fry up worked wonders this morning, but I'm still restricting the night's drinking to a glass of wine with dinner. I'd only brought two dresses with me, which helped with the decision making. Laura, my teacher friend who organised this weekend, agreed to meet me before the meal so I wouldn't be walking into the restaurant by myself.

I've not told anyone about my past here, about the fact that I found my ex-boyfriend playing the faithful and doting father yesterday. It's a painful truth that I hope I never have to share with anyone. My plan is to meet Laura and my other old friends, have a nice meal and nostalgic evening (as much as my stomach will allow) and then drive back to Ipswich and lick my wounds once again, as if I'm doomed to repeat my past forever.

I look up from my thoughts to see Laura standing in front of me. She looks stunning in a green dress that compliments her curly, long red hair. She seems to have achieved what I'd wished for, and now realise that I failed at.

"Hi Kate, you look lovely" She says, obviously trying to be nice.

I glance back into the mirror at the auburn hair that has now crept down almost to my shoulders. It suited me as a messy cropped cut, but my few years of self-neglect have proved that it shouldn't have been allowed to grow longer. Teamed with the dowdy knee length black dress – that I wince to remember Ali making me buy in the Christmas sale, purely because it's colour meant it was the only thing I'd try on – I look tired and like I'm trying hard to be something I'm not.

"It's been so long since we've seen you!" Laura exclaims, drawing me into a slightly awkward hug.

"I know, I've been back at home for a while, just catching up. Thanks for inviting me" I offer back, wondering whether my stomach will allow me to drink more than I'd planned to get through whatever questions are thrown my way.

Millie

Sam had been so upset when we got back that I'd suggested we ask Alex if we could pick Mae up and bring her to us for the night. It's something that we'd never done before, but Mae knew us well by now, so an overnight stay should be fine. Plus, this gave Sam the option to wallow in her room while I amused Mae with the Lion King, Little Mermaid, and whatever other delights Alex had in their collection.

Sam is asleep when we arrive at Alex's flat, so I offer him the bullet points of our day, while filling the car with all of the paraphernalia needed to entertain a baby for a night. When he's kissed Mae goodnight – promising to call before bedtime as he fixes the car seat into the back of Sam's car – he begins a long list of numbers and tips as I usher him out towards the flat.

"Alex?" I interrupt him, smiling.

"Yes?" He asks, handing me a piece of paper with emergency details on that I recognise as the one they usually keep on the fridge.

"We love her, she'll be fine" I blow him a kiss and close the car door with a smile.

Ruby

I'll admit I was a bit concerned for Mae to be spending the night away, but as it was last minute, and it's our closest friends, I'm just happy to be spending the evening with Alex.

While he dealt with packing Mae's overnight bag, I finished getting ready, putting on the blue dress that he picked out just after we became parents. It's long and has a rippling neck and when I wear it – on special occasions – I feel as special as I did when I pulled back the changing room curtain. I'd not long lost the baby weight and for the first time since pregnancy, I saw the desire in his eyes as he saw the curve of my tummy. I'd worked hard to get rid of the bump and his eyes simply mimicked the expression that they'd had on our first night together. Needless to say, I was happy and relieved. The dress had become my lucky dress, and I hoped that tonight it would help to take us away from ear infections, deadlines and everything in between so we could get back to us.

Just us.

I love our family, but I want Alex to myself sometimes, so he can remember the woman that he fell in love with rather than the mother and the partner in life.

Sam

I wake up, feeling a bit hazy. I can see cars whizzing past and can hear Millie and Mae singing something I recognise from a Disney film.

"Hey sleepy face, you OK?" Millie asks, before joining Mae for a hearty but confused chorus that I realise is from the Lion King.

I nod, rubbing sleep from eyes and pulling the fold-out mirror towards me to discover that my hair – currently fading from a coppery colour – has flattened on one side where I've slept against the window. I have no time to correct this though, as my phone starts to ring in my pocket. I see Alex's name on the display and hope we haven't left something behind.

"Sam? Thank God – I forgot to put Mae's cuddly frog, Freddy, into the bag. It's her favourite toy, she won't sleep without it. She'd taken it out to play with while I was packing! I'm so sorry, would you be able to come back and get it?" Alex sounds panicked, so I assure him that we'll turn around. I hang up and explain to Millie, who sighs but indicates to turn around and we head back for Freddy the Frog.

Alex

After I hang up from Sam, I turn to open the bedroom door and Ruby's stood in the hallway ready for me.

She's wearing that dress, my favourite, and I feel my heart lift in a weird way that makes me confident and sure of what I want to do tonight.

I offered to drive us into Winchester, knowing I didn't want to get drunk and make a mess of what I'd got planned. Plus, I wanted Ruby to have a glass or two of wine and enjoy what I hoped would be a night she'd look back on and remember for the rest of her life. If I get the answer I'm hoping for, of course.

We arrive at Pizza Express and take our seats, ordering some wine as I try to conjure up the confidence I'd felt in the car and remember the plan I'd had for how the evening would progress.

"Are you alright babe?" Ruby asks me, looking in concern as she accepts a glass of red from the waitress.

"I'm fine" I say, shrugging off my coat and accepting a menu. How does anyone ever relax enough to do this?

"Do you want to share a starter?" She asks, leaning across the table, glass in hand.

"If you like" I say, smiling at her, loving how she can ease my mood with a look.

I let her choose the starter, realising that selecting a main course will use as much brain power as I have. I hope this goes to plan, taking another long swig of water. Ruby pours a small amount of red into my glass, but I know it's best to stay clear headed for the time being.

Kate

We walk into the restaurant, Laura already spotting the group and waving as we walk towards the table.

As we sashay amongst the other diners, my worst fears are realised and I feel the blood chill in my veins. Alex and Ruby are here.

I take a deep breath and hope that they don't see me, and perhaps my back will be towards them when I'm sat down. We get to our table, and the only two spare chairs are facing inwards. I smile to the familiar faces that feel like I knew them a lifetime ago, and sit down. Directly in my eye line, though on the opposite side of the room, are Ruby and my ex-boyfriend. The love of my life, having dinner with the girl that he swore for years was his best friend and nothing more.

I wonder how many times they laughed about it, how many stories he told her of the two of us in intimate scenarios. I find my gaze drawn to them, watching the way she talks and leans across the table to show him something on the menu. Was the child really theirs? Have they made a whole life without me, after he promised me that he loved me for seven years?

"Kate, are you OK?" Laura nudges me, gesturing towards another girl – Nicole? Anna? – who has asked me a question. I bring myself back to the group, knowing I need to distract myself.

"Sorry, I'm a bit hung over. What did I miss?" I smile as the line I hoped would work results in a round of knowing laughter.

Millie

We arrive back at Alex's flat just as Mae has fallen asleep.

I get out of the car, glad that I'm tall enough to retrieve the emergency key from its place on top of the stone block that sits above the front door frame. I open the door and see Freddy sat on the table that houses the phone and a few unopened letters. Underneath the frog lies a note:

Sorry, can't believe I forgot to pack Freddy! I owe you both a drink, wish me luck, Alex x

I can't help but smile, holding a soft frog with a cheeky sewn tongue hanging from his mouth, whilst thinking how happy Ruby will be when they arrive back at home.

I tuck the note into my jeans and lock the door behind me, walking back to the car to find Sam smiling through the tears that have crept back into those sad, pretty eyes.

Kate

I've been in a conversation with Naomi, a girl from my course that I had almost forgotten. We'd been discussing teaching, as she's also teaching English.

My attention is pulled away, almost snapped away, as I sip my wine and glance over towards the table that breaks my heart.

Our table had just ordered dessert, though I'd opted out, and I see that Alex and Ruby have chosen to share. Some kind of generic cheesecake arrives at their table, and I blink as Alex places a small black box on the table.

Really?!

He says nothing, but keeps it under his napkin, and I can sense that she hasn't seen it yet. Once again, I can tell what he's going to do before she does.

I know I can't watch this.

Feeling glad that I've not had more than a glass, I suddenly apologise and stand up, feigning my hangover resurfacing, and struggle to reach the door without raising suspicion.

I need to go home, now. I need to be with my sister and try to forget the last few days. Ali was wrong, my friends were wrong. I shouldn't have come back, but I did and now I have to leave.

As I walk hurriedly to my car, I pull my phone

out of my bag and type a quick text to Ali to let her know how hellish my evening became and that I'll be home early.

It's started to rain, and I reach up to pull a few straggly strands of hair out of my eyes. I don't remember ever feeling quite so desolate and pathetic, and I can't believe that when I'd come here in search of closure I'd stumbled back upon the two people I least wanted to find, while they were at their happiest. My stomach churns and I turn on the engine, determined to get home before I drive myself crazy over all of the time I've wasted on such a doomed relationship.

Ben

In the end I decided to drive down and see Sam face to face, knowing she couldn't hang up a phone or ignore me in the flesh.

I feel like I've been driving for hours to get to her flat, but as I pull off the M3 and follow the signs to Winchester; I think I spot her car. I'm momentarily confused, thinking that she must have been home hours ago, but as I switch lanes and settle in behind her little Mini, it's obviously her and Millie in the front seats . . . I've struck gold.

I'm undecided whether to follow them home, or whether to flash my lights and see if they pull over. It's risky, but if we reach their flat, they can always slam the door in my face.

I follow them closely for just under a mile, before I flash my lights and wait to see what Sam will do.

Ruby

"Wow, this cheesecake is amazing!" I say as I dive in again with my fork.

Alex has been weird and restless all night. He's been attentive, but flustered. He hardly touched his pasta, and now has left me to eat much more than half of the dessert.

"Babe, what's going on with you tonight?" I reach across to him, and as I touch his elbow, he flinches and I see a familiar little box rock on the table.

"Alex?" I look up at him, confused.

"Ruby-"His smile falters as he pulls his hand from mine and reaches into his pocket for his vibrating phone.

As soon as he answers, I know something's wrong. I've only had a few small glasses of wine but the night has suddenly taken a few turns that I can't quite process. His face moves from concerned to angry, to panicked in a few short moments. He hangs up and puts the box back into his pocket.

"Ruby, I'm sorry, that was Sam. She was upset, but said something about being followed in the car. Mae's with them, we need to find them" His tone makes me lock eyes with the nearest waiter, leave some money on the table and grab for my coat.

Kate

I can't believe what I've just seen, and feel sick as I get into my car and pull out onto the street.

The amount of one way streets don't help, and I force myself to concentrate on the road as I speed back towards home, knowing I need to leave this life behind and make my own count.

I had plugged in the sat nav, but it always takes a few minutes to kick in and realise where it is. Luckily I remember most of the journey so I plough on, hoping that the roads will disappear behind me like the life I could have had.

I turn the stereo up, switching radio stations until I hear some generic dance music to grab my attention with its repetitive beat. I open the window, letting in some air to keep me alert and prepare me for the motorway journey.

I change lanes, getting lost in a world of my own delayed heartbreak, as I see a bright light dart across my path. I try to swerve and push my horn, but it's too late, I hear screaming metal and a mechanical orchestra of horns.

Then nothing but darkness.

Sam

"Are you sure that's Ben's car?" Millie asks, her voice sounding panicked as I squint into the rear view mirror.

"Yeah, it's him. What the hell is he doing?" I reply, my heart starting to beat fast as I hang up the phone. Perhaps I shouldn't have phoned Alex, but Ben's Mazda has been following us closely for at least a few miles and has flashed us a few times. Honestly, I'm not sure what he's trying to do.

"Should I pull over?!" Millie cries, glancing into the back seat to make sure we've not woken Mae.

"No, just keep driving. If we ignore him, surely he'll give up?" I turn in my seat, seeing the beams of Ben's car a few feet behind. I don't know what he's playing at, but he won't stop.

We pull up at a deserted set of traffic lights. As soon as it turns to green, Millie drives off but Ben becomes more insistent. He sounds his horn a few times, luckily not waking Mae who looks adorable asleep with a head of dark brown curls creeping onto her shoulders. I stick my hand out of the window, giving him a rude but necessary signal to back off. He stays back until we reach a dual carriageway.

He pulls up parallel to Millie's car and starts to shout through the window. I can't hear what he's saying, but I know the road reduces back to a single road after less than a mile so I decide to ignore him.

Ben has finally started to slow down, his car almost behind ours. Suddenly though, there is a loud horn and more headlights as another car collides with his, sending a sickening sound of twisting metal towards us.

Ben

I can smell burning.

I open my eyes, struggling to realise what's in front of me. I can see my body, all functioning and moving as I test it. My car has seen better days, but looks driveable.

I start to open my door, seeing a random girl in the car that I somehow collided with. She's stirring, so I keep looking. My breath catches in my throat as I look at the other car and feel sick to my stomach.

Sam and Millie are both unconscious in the front, while I suddenly see Mae – Alex's daughter whom I'd met only a few times – asleep in a car seat in the back. My body begins to shake as I realise what I've done.

Something kicks into me, some force of panic or practicality and I walk past the random girl.

"Please call an ambulance" I say to her horror as I get back into my car and reverse, watching that no other cars are behind me.

I can't be here, and I know that Sam won't ever want to lay eyes on me again. I drive as quickly as I can, towards Bristol and away from a woman that I'll need to forget about if I want to sleep through the night again.

Alex

We drive through the quiet roads, looking for a sign of Millie's car.

The night is getting dark, but all of a sudden we drive past a police car and an ambulance.

"Alex" Ruby's voice is breathless, her mind working out what I'm too scared to contemplate.

We park up and walk up to the accident: Two cars looking worse for wear and I realise with dread that the Sam's Mini is one of them. It looks written off, and I can see paramedics trying to cut someone from the drivers' seat.

We approach an ambulance, almost too scared to see what we'll find. A female paramedic is working on a child, and both of us break into a run to locate our baby.

"Excuse me Miss, you need to step back" Says a male police officer, putting a hand on Ruby's arm.

"No! Is that Mae?" Ruby's voice cracks and the tears seem to inform the police man that we're authorised. Ruby runs into the ambulance, and I can see her trying not to cry as she sees our baby having treatment.

"Is she OK?" I ask the paramedic, looking down at Mae, whose face is covered in blood.

"She's stable for now, but I need to get her to the hospital. Are you her parents?"

"Yes" I hear Ruby say as my eyes wander to the other car. My heart falls into my shoes as I tell Ruby I'll meet her at the hospital.

I'm transfixed by a familiar car from a lifetime ago, and it has taken my breath away. There is another paramedic talking to the driver, using words like 'intent' and 'warrant'. I barely hear him as I make my way round towards the car, needing to prove my instincts wrong.

I make out the face that has haunted my dreams for a long time, and decide to get my revenge if she has had anything to do with harming my child. I say her name, not expecting her to meet my eyes with such fear and contempt.

"Kate?"

Ruby

I've been sat in a plastic chair with blue frayed fabric cushioning for almost two hours.

My patience is wearing thin and no one will tell me what's going on. I want to see my child; I need to know that Mae is OK, and that my family are going to be able to go home and wake up to normality tomorrow.

Alex arrived about an hour ago but hasn't really said anything. His complexion is pasty, as I'm sure mine is, but he's been restless and refused to even share a coffee with me.

Nurses and doctors keep walking out of the doors to deliver different kinds of news. Will we be one of the lucky ones, told that things were tough but our little fighter pulled through and we can take her home? Or will the doctor push through the swinging doors, with that horrific generic saddened expression on his face?

Either way the waiting is driving me insane: I need to know one way or the other. What started out as such a lovely, romantic evening has turned into a nightmare.

Sam

I'm not sure I've ever felt worse.

My memory of the last few hours is hazy – the nurse said it should return quickly, when the shock starts to fade – but I woke up to find that Millie was nowhere in sight.

I asked the nurse where my best friend was, and all I got in response was a headshake and a pat on the shoulder. I'd been told to stay overnight after suffering a few bruised ribs, but I needed to know what was going on.

I put my bag on my shoulder with a wince and made my way to the reception desk.

"Excuse me; I'm looking for Amelia Taylor?" I ask, looking up at the male nurse with what I hope are puppy dog eyes.

"Taylor?" He scans his computer screen, frowning until my nurse nudges him and whispers in his ear.

"I'm sorry hun, I believe she was involved in a car collision earlier on. She's still in the Intensive Care Unit, but there should be more news soon" He gives me a look of concern and offers me a seat as I feel the wind get kicked out of me.

"Can I ring someone for you?" He asks, but I shake my head: I imagine that my friends are already here.

"Take me to the waiting room please" I ask,

my mind trying to catch up with what's happening.

Alex and Ruby will be here, I vaguely remember ringing him. I told him we were being followed, knowing he would help. As I walk towards the waiting room, I close my eyes, seeing Mae's face with headlights shining out behind her. I shake my head to clear it of the night's confusion, and it's only as I find my friend's sat in the seats that I realise that this night has potentially ruined everything.

Ruby

I feel like I'm going out of my mind.

Alex and I have been sat in this waiting room for hours, waiting for some strange doctor to come and tell us whether our child has survived. I don't remember ever feeling this disjointed, as if my brain and my body are separate and both need comprehension from the truth before they can join up again.

Alex is sat next to me, his hand over my shoulder – slightly limp from fatigue – and I look to him now, just as his eyes jolt up towards the door. I follow his gaze, and see a young nurse walking through to speak to us.

"Miss. Walker?" She asks, approaching us with a look of caution.

"Ruby, please, and this is Alex. How is our daughter?" I hear the fear in my voice, and Alex's hand on my back tells me he can hear it too.

"She's stable for the moment. Would you both like to follow me into the family waiting room?" We follow her, Sam walking quietly behind us.

"Mae is a fighter, but she lost some blood at the scene. We need to take some blood from each of you to replenish her for recovery. Would that be OK?" Before the nurse has finished, Alex and I are both on our feet.

"Please, take it. Whatever she needs" Alex has

rolled up his sleeve, panic and tiredness acting on his behalf. The nurse gives a polite smile.

"Give me five minutes, I'll be back with the tools I need to take the blood" and with that, she slips out of the glass doors.

Alex

The nurse took our blood a few hours ago, and we've been sat in this goldfish bowl of a room ever since, hoping that our baby will survive this horrible ordeal.

The nurse suddenly slinks back into the room, taking Ruby to one side and whispering to her in hushed tones. Ruby shakes her head and gestures to me, the two of them walking up to the sofas where I've been sitting and trying not to fidget.

"There's news on Mae" Ruby says to me, reaching out to hold my hand. We both look up at the nurse hopefully.

"As I said to Miss. Walker, while Mae is stable and recovering, this news is somewhat delicate" Her eyes flash towards Ruby.

"It's fine. Anything you have to say can be said to us both" Ruby replies.

"Well, as you know, I took your blood in order to help Mae's recovery. All blood taken from donors has to be tested so we know it's free from infection and is safe for the recipient" The nurse pauses here, apparently choosing her words carefully.

"Ruby, your blood type is A. Alex is AB. Mae is type O. I'm afraid that's not possible. Ruby can't take the blood, and we'll need to find another source. I'm sorry"

I struggle to fathom what I'm being told, and vaguely hear Sam offering her arm to be tested as my girlfriend collapses gently to the floor.

2007: (3 Years Earlier)

Ruby

Amy's been flirting with the barman for about an hour now, and I'm bored. I got bored with the cocktails too, after Chris – the barman – decided to reserve the free drinks for my best friend who would make it worth his while. I wave to her that I need some air, but she's too busy fluttering her eyelids to see me.

I wander outside, checking my phone to realise it's past midnight. There are no texts from Alex, though there's not much reception either. I sit down on the bench, though the day's rain makes this short lived and I look up at the stars instead. I hear a cough behind me that becomes a slight whimper. I turn round to see Luke in the archway between the pub and the small cinema beside it. He's sat on the floor, obviously a bit worse for wear, but I could never stand to see him cry.

"Luke?" I whisper, moving towards him.

He looks up, his face darkening as he sees mine.

"What?" He asks, forcing himself up to standing. He reaches his hand out for the wall, but misses and his shoulder hits the brick with a painful thud.

"Are you ok?" I ask, knowing this is a pointless question. He's obviously drunk and morose.

"Do you care?" He raises an eyebrow, turning round and walking through the archway to the darkness behind.

"Of course I care, wait!" If nothing else, I owe him a shoulder to cry on. I feel guilty for what I put him through, even though he once scared me more than anyone else has.

"What, Ruby? Wait for you to tell me it's going to be alright? To tell me that you're not living with my best friend after you cheated on me with him? "His laugh is bitter, just like his tone of voice. He looks me straight in the eye and I look away, suddenly uneasy.

"Luke, I'm sorry. I know things didn't work out well for us. I know that was partly my fault, but you have to move on" I try to touch his shoulder, but he flinches away.

"Move on, like you have? Tell me one thing, Ruby. Did you ever love me? I mean, the way you love him" His voice cracks on the last few words and I feel that I should make amends somehow.

"Of course I loved you Luke, we were together for years. You were the first person I ever loved" I tell him, seeing him smile slightly. I move to walk away, thinking I've said enough.

"So, what was it about him that stole you away?" His voice is soft now, his fingers tracing my cheek. I can smell the alcohol on his breath, and feel the overwhelming need to turn away.

"Was it the passion you felt for him? I saw the two of you, remember. I'd not seen you look at me like that for so long. Like you needed me right then and there" His grasp of my cheek becomes tight, his eyes close as I realise he's trying to kiss me.

"Luke, stop it!" I try to move away, but he's always been much stronger than me.

His hands move into my hair, pulling the roots painfully into his fists. His mouth opens on mine, and his tongue pushes my lips apart. I try to wriggle away, but he grabs my wrists and, as I attempt to move, we tumble to the floor.

I open my eyes, feeling groggy and sore.

I look around, trying to gather my bearings, but its dark and raining and I feel a rising sense of panic in my chest. My clutch bag is lying next to me, closed and apparently undisturbed. My head hurts and a quick touch to my temple reveals that I'm bleeding slightly.

Nothing else seems to be damaged, though my pelvis feels a bit sore, so I attempt to stand and figure out where the hell I am. I'm stood in a dingy alleyway, but as I stumble back out to the street I realise I'm not lost.

I'm standing in front of a familiar pub, knowing that Millie's shop is just around the corner. I sigh with relief as I realise I can get myself home. I take my phone out of my bag and see that the display reads 04:36. I vaguely remember having a few drinks with Amy, but that was hours ago. The silent and dark streets make me nervous and I quicken my pace to reach the train station. Luckily I arrive just five minutes before the train that will take me back to Alex and the safety of his warm embrace.

I let myself into the flat, having had almost half an hour to worry about how I came to wake up in a deserted alleyway. How I was fairly unhurt and not mugged I'm not sure. Maybe it was an attempted mugging and they were interrupted? Whatever it was, I need Alex to comfort me after this bizarre night.

I can hear the TV blaring before I see my boyfriend: Seemingly passed out on the sofa with a half empty vodka bottle on the coffee table. I know he'd got into the habit of drinking too much while I was away, but I thought that was all done with now we were together. Perhaps that's a naive hope, but this obviously wasn't just a few drinks at the end of a bad day.

I decide to give him the benefit of the doubt, feeling almost guilty given that I'd woken up with little memory of last night. I nudge him, but the only response is a sleepy whimper as he turns over onto his front. Watching him sleep, I'm suddenly overcome with tiredness. I slip under the covers of our bed, relishing the feeling of normality that this brings.

The last hour has been odd and unsettling, and I'm so happy and relieved to be home and in my own bed. I close my eyes and fall into a deep sleep full of troublesome dreams.

Millie

Once again I find myself in my office before 8am, glad that I switched to lemonade last night while Sam and Luke continued with the cocktails.

I'd been so relieved to have Luke's help, so I was surprised and disappointed to find an email from him this morning. It had been sent late last night, apologetic and briefly explaining his need to return home for some family emergency. He'd be able to help from there if needed he assured me, though it would have been much more helpful to have him here to go through his notes again. I wasn't being fair of course: I replied gratefully, sending my wishes to his family and thanking him for his help so far.

I've been sat in front of Luke's notes for the past hour, and have driven myself slightly stir crazy with number crunching and attempting to embrace the facts and figures.

I need more caffeine, I realise with a large and satisfying stretch. I walk through the archway to my tiny but cosy kitchenette and turn the kettle on. As I wait for it to boil, I amble through my shop, reminding myself why I need to save it. Looking around at the tables of beads, and outside at the early morning sunshine shining through my windows, I feel a sense of achievement and happiness. I know I need to get this right: To honour my Nan's memory and her belief in me, and to prove to myself that this can be a success.

I pour my coffee and then sit down again with Luke's notes. There's a section on cost cutting and financial advice, and also notes from a brainstorming session that we had for ways to grow the business and promote it to the community. This included craft workshops and 'social networking'. I laugh as I remember the confused frown on my face at this point in the session. Luke grinned at me and suggested I get some tips from Sam.

I send her a quick text suggesting we meet for lunch, and then settle myself to read through the financial advice once again. If I'm going to save my beloved shop, I need to get this stuff into my head and make it work.

Alex

I can hear music, and my head is rebelling against it.

I try to turn over, but there's sunlight and my eyes refuse to let it in. Instead, I turn back onto my stomach and breathe deeply in an attempt to stop my hangover from taking over my whole body.

"Babe, are you awake?" I hear Ruby's voice whisper in my ear. All I can do is groan and close my eyes against the day.

"Looks like you had a heavy night in?" Her tone is concerned, but I can't summon the brain power to process how best to react. I hear her sigh and am relieved when she strokes my arm and stands up.

"My mum phoned earlier. She'd booked a few days away in Brighton with my dad but he's got a business trip. She asked me to go with her. Do you mind? I'll be back tomorrow night" I force myself to turn over and face her.

She's smiling, but her face is tight and she looks exhausted. I know she misses her mum and don't want her to feel she needs to stay to nurse my hangover. I'd planned to have one or two shots to take the edge off the disappointment that she'd gone out rather than come home to me. I can only blame myself for the fact that my first response to a night home alone is apparently to drink myself into a stupor. But as everyone knows, the fact that a hangover is self-inflicted just makes the pain worse.

"Of course I don't mind Ruby, go and have fun with your mum and then come home so we can celebrate your job properly" I smile, accept the kiss on my temple and then turn back over to relieve the nausea as she pads into the bedroom to pack.

Sam

I came into work early this morning – the joys of management – to make sure that Nick had left things in order ready for the lunchtime rush.

Luckily he had, so I cleaned the tables down and sat in a corner booth to brainstorm about new menu ideas. We only really offer snacks and the odd sandwich, and I've been pushing head office to look into a snack bar to help us pull in the lunch time customers. To be honest, it would also help us to suggest a bit of damage control in the evenings when groups of students come in and there's not much on offer to absorb all the drinks.

I love managing the bar, but have so many ideas for how to grow the chain and make things more interesting. For a start, there used to be small local gigs here when I first became bar staff, but these have been kept to a minimum in the last year. I'm not sure whose idea that was, but it's resulted in a lot less custom. I've been told that if I want to organise performances, I'm allowed to trial it. I plan to do this, and have been on the lookout for local bands, advertising in the window and through some contacts that I found through old course friends. I've had a bit of interest, though nothing concrete yet.

I look down at my notepad, reading the scribbles about menu and gig ideas. It makes my mind wander to Millie, having the courage to go it alone and start up her own business. Sometimes it feels like this is my own little bar, but I can only dream of the reality that comes with what Millie's taken on. There's a quiet knock on the window and I look up to see her face: My best friend looks tired but excited. I get up and unlock the door, kissing her cheek and bringing her back to the booth where my notepad is strewn across the table.

"Did you hear from Luke after he disappeared last night?" I ask, my puzzled expression mirrored on her face.

"Actually yes, he sent me an email. Apparently he had to go back home for a family emergency" She uses air quotes for this, "but he's emailed me some more tips and said I should reply with questions"

"That's a shame, I hope everything's OK. Do you have enough tips to go on for the shop?" I smile as she produces her laptop.

"I've been brainstorming and have some ideas about workshops and things I can do to get people through the door. I need your help though" Millie's excitement is infectious, and I nod as I look at the screen to see what she's been planning.

Ruby

I board the train, excited to spend a few days by the beach with my mum, who I haven't seen much in the last few years.

It feels a bit unnatural, having been so close to her, to be living so far away now. We still talk every few days, but it's not quite the same as popping round to see her and share my day.

She met Alex when we were housemates at University, and she took an immediate shine to him. She's never been judgemental about our friendship the way other people were, and she didn't understand Kate's lack of interest in socialising with us.

Mum was the first person I rang when things came to a head with Luke and she and Alex are still the only two people that know that Luke hit me. I was embarrassed and ashamed of what had happened, but she made me see that it wasn't completely my fault. I have some amazing friends – Sam and Millie especially – but I can never confide in anyone quite like my mother.

I look out of the train window, watching the fields and sheep rush by, and try to clear my head after the last few days. I've not yet talked to mum much about my new job as I wanted to tell her in person. After the few hours of sleep I had this morning, my head feels cloudy and unreliable. I don't really remember anything from last night, but I'm hoping that talking to mum with a glass of wine on the beach will help refresh me so we can celebrate my new job offer. After travelling for so long, mum was concerned that I'd struggled to find work so I can't wait to tell her.

Alex

Ruby must have left a while ago, but I seem to have lost all concept of time.

I roll over and stand up, knowing that I need to face this hangover rather than sleep until it passes. I feel like I have let Ruby down by letting her see me like this, after finally changing my ways since we got together.

I pour myself some coffee and then inspect the fridge for a possible lunch idea. I feel triumphant when I see there are sufficient ingredients for a bacon sandwich and the fact that I don't run to the bathroom with this thought makes me perk up even more.

After lunch, a shower makes me feel slightly more human, and I saunter back through the flat to try and figure out what to do with my day. I'm not back at work until tomorrow evening, which now feels frustrating with Ruby away for the whole time.

My eyes rest on the CD player, and I remember that Kate bought this for me one Christmas after we'd had a huge argument. The thought of her, and our failed relationship, make me suddenly realise how much I want to make things work with Ruby. Kate and I were together for more years than I care to remember, but when I think of her I think of a comfortable companionship. We had a lot of fun in the early years, and I never doubted that I loved her, but I don't remember feeling the passion that Ruby and I share. Perhaps it's a result of feeling an attraction when it's forbidden, which I finally admitted to Ruby during one of our first nights together. We'd made love a few times by then, and it had already been more passionate than any intimacy that Kate and I had shared. I'm not proud to admit to falling in love with someone when I was still with someone else, but sometimes these things happen and I can only take comfort and strength from the way Ruby and I finally got our chance.

I select my favourite REM album – Automatic for the People – and give in to the relaxed familiarity of the lyrics as I walk around the room. I decide to clean up and make the flat look it's best for Ruby's return. I could even go out tomorrow and buy some flowers to leave for her to find when she gets home.

Firstly, I make myself another coffee and sit down to think of ways to make my girlfriend smile as she walks through the door after a few days by the beach.

Millie

It's almost noon as I wander around my little shop with a smile of productive satisfaction.

It's Sunday, a day I usually take as my own to spend with Sam or home alone watching films while she scuttles off to Ben's. Today though, I have been working hard to reorganise the layout of the shop to cater for workshops.

Sam helped me to think of ideas for family days and kid's events: Showing people how to make jewellery and encouraging the community to be creative with the tools I have available. It will mean buying in a few more beads for them to use, but it will be more than worth it if we can bring more custom in and get people excited to do some crafting.

It's something I didn't really think about, but Sam helped me to set up a Face book page, and I've already got over 100 likes after less than a week. I suppose I have Sam to thank for that – She has a crazy amount of followers when you combine her personal page and her Night Light persona. She shared my advert around so many people that I now apparently have a fan in Switzerland.

I have bought a large round table from the local DIY shop and some pretty chairs that we found in a scrap yard. Sam and Ben were once again on hand to help me sand and paint the chairs into different bright colours, bringing a quirky but inviting look to the back of the shop. Sam will come in later to help me do some promotion – I'm still a bit useless with the whole online thing – but she's promised to teach me enough that I'll be able to interact with customers and set up events. I'm sure it'll take more than a few workshops to get myself into profit but it's a start, and one that I'm getting more excited about each day.

Ruby

I see mum's face from the train and feel immediately better when it breaks into a beam at the sight of her little girl.

After a long cuddle, she takes my bag and begins to walk it to the entrance of the station. She chatters to me nonstop with a catch up of her life since our last phone call: Annoyance that my dad was called away on business to London at a moment's notice, excitement that it meant she got me to herself for a few days instead. We're out of the taxi and into the hotel before she has so much as taken a breath.

I look into her eyes and she smiles, finally inhaling and then laughing at her own over excitement. She's wearing a knee length blue dress with silver buttons down the front of it, which almost looks denim but has a more luxurious texture. Her hair was the same colour as mine when I was little, but she has dyed it red for the last decade at least. The vibrancy of it suits her personality, and she's recently had it cut from shoulder length to where it is now, brushing her chin in a chic bob. She has several bracelets rattling on her wrists, and her pointy black ankle boots clip-clop up the hotel steps as she sashays in ahead of me.

I'm reminded how much of a welcome

distraction my mum can be from the everyday grind of life, and I relax as she takes control of everything. We're soon out of reception having dropped my bags off, and walking towards the pier. I feel the sea air and take a deep breath. The cold, damp saltiness fills my lungs and brings more wellbeing to my body.

We walk down the stone steps, enjoying the sound of the energetic waves, and crunch along the stones on the way to a seafront bar that we used to come to on weekends when I was at University. Mum orders us some wine without needing to check my preference and we find an empty table where we can catch up properly as we watch the water dance.

Sam

I reach across the bar to hand Ben his pint.

He agreed to come in to see me at work tonight to help me brainstorm some ideas for the bar, in return for a few drinks and perhaps a few sexual favours when we close.

"So, you want to bring back the acoustic music?" He asks, obviously quite happy about my idea.

"Yeah, it was one of my favourite things when I started working here and I want to bring it back. Not many places offer free gigs" I follow him to a corner booth, looking up as a random blonde girl shouts a greeting to my boyfriend. He nods at her, but has the good grace to blush as I catch his eye. She looks familiar, but I can't place her, so choose to ignore her instead.

"So, how easy do you think it will be to get the music thing up and running?" He asks, sitting down and pulling me towards him on the seat.

"I don't know, I've emailed a few of my course contacts and have advertised for some new local bands that would be interested to perform for free" I giggle as his hands tickle my hips.

"OK, that's a good start. Perhaps the local paper, or even through Facebook?" Ben smiles as I feel my face lighting up.

This is achievable – I could make changes

here. The idea fills me with an excitement that I suddenly realise is infectious as Ben catches my eye and gives me a look I've come to know well. He leans over for a kiss, his hand resting on my stomach before it starts to creep upwards.

"Ben – "I manage, pulling away as I smile at him.

"Sorry, you're working. Maybe when you close?" He raises an eyebrow and smiles as I stand up, laughing as I wink and walk back to the bar.

Ruby

Mum and I have been shopping for most of the afternoon.

We finally decide to rest for a late lunch in a pub on the seafront, when Mum can no longer carry the bags she's accumulated so far. She orders two large glasses of wine and a bowl of chips to share as I grab a table and let our bags fall by my feet.

"Well, we've done well so far!" She laughs as I survey our purchases with disbelief.

"I thought my two bags were bad, but you've bought the whole city!" I giggle, accepting the wine that the waitress puts in front of me.

"We needed some retail therapy, and we definitely need wine" She chinks her glass to mine and takes a long sip.

"So, how are things with Alex?" Her smile grows, wanting details of romance from me while my dad is away.

"They're fine" I try to elaborate, but the last few days gets stuck in my throat.

"Just fine? What's wrong darling?" She puts her glass down and leans towards me.

"Nothing really, we've just had a strange week" I sigh and relay the last few days to her, not sure of how it will sound to someone else. When I try to explain the previous night I stumble on my words, scared to admit that I'm not sure what actually happened. Mum's frown deepens at this point, a look of shock and concern on her face as I brush my hair from my forehead and she sees the slight graze.

"Do you remember how you got into the alleyway?" She asks, her hand reaching across to hold mine.

"Not really, I remember meeting Amy and then . . . "I close my eyes, urging a memory to come forward.

"I saw Luke" I say suddenly, my head jerking up to see Mum looking at me intently.

"You saw him in the bar?"

"No, I came outside. He was there, but that's all I remember. I woke up this morning and felt so strange" I put my fingers through my hair, looking up to see tears in my mum's eyes.

I feel a chill that seems to run through my bones, up my spine and through to my shoulders, making me shiver.

"Look, Mum. I'm fine, let's not dampen the shopping mood. Where else do you want to go?" I take a chip, then lift my glass up to realise I've somehow already drained the contents.

Alex

I decide to get rid of all the alcohol we have in the flat.

I'm not in need of rehabilitation, but I don't want to get to that point. I want to be good enough for Ruby, and for that I need to look after myself.

There's only a bottle and a half of vodka – my old emergency stash – and less than half a bottle of red wine. I'll get a new bottle of wine for when she returns, but I need to know I can have a night alone without getting drunk. I pour away the wine and the almost-empty vodka bottle, placing the glass in the recycling box under the sink. I hold the remaining bottle in my hand for a moment, wanting it out of sight but feeling it would be a waste to throw it away. I grab an empty storage box from on top of the corner cupboard and place the bottle inside, pushing the lid down with a satisfying click and replacing the box on top of the cupboard where it's hard to reach and won't be a temptation.

I've got some films ready to watch, and have dinner in the oven, but I resolve to remain on water for the night so that I can be fresh and ready for Ruby tomorrow.

I'd watched the vodka running into the sink, ironically looking like water. The innocence of its appeal can't fool me anymore; I'm not sure I could count how many times it took me away from reality and lowered me down into a pile of self-hatred.

I flick through the DVD collection, alighting on Face Off – A film that Ruby and I have watched together countless times. I take my dinner through to the lounge and sit down to try and enjoy the first sober night home alone that I can remember.

Millie

This is incredible.

I took some photos of my newly updated shop and used them to update my new online shop profile – with help from Sam of course. She's been here all day – Another tiring but productive Sunday. We've posted photos of the beads and products I've made, as well as the shop and a few of us both being silly for what she called the 'approachable, personable edge'.

We're now sat at my desk, watching as new people 'share' and 'like' my products. My company 'likes' have grown way past what I thought possible already, and I even let Sam start to play with her own profile. She moves the mouse as she scrolls down the screen, frowning as something catches her eye.

"What's wrong?" I ask, leaning forward to look at the highlighted photo.

"Do you remember that random blonde girl that I told you talked to Ben the other night?" Her voice is rising with each word.

"It's Amy, the girl who slept with Alex" She almost laughs as she clicks on a photo. I follow her eye line and see the caption: **'me and my ex finally catching up over breakfast'** with some kind of sickening cheeky face after the text.

"Ben went out with Amy?!" I ask, trying not

to laugh at the strange coincidence.

"My guess is that she counted a one night stand as a relationship" Sam laughs, but I can see surprise and worry in her face.

"Ask Ben about it, I'm sure it's nothing" I say, pulling the laptop back out of her view as I close down the internet. We've done enough for today, given it's a day off for both of us. It's time for our weekly treat – Sunday lunch at our favourite pub. I even get a smile from Sam as I offer to buy hers, and we race each other to the bar.

Ruby

I'm suddenly feeling a bit lost and homesick.

I left Mum at the station about half an hour ago, after a wonderful few days with her by the beach. We've always loved Brighton and I really miss her in between visits. Whether it's the flush of a new relationship I'm not sure, but I'm happy to be heading back to Alex.

I do still feel a bit confused, but something in my brain refuses to let me see the full picture, so I reach into my bag and bring out the sandwich Mum bought me before I boarded the train. I decide not to let uncertainty encroach on my life, especially now that Alex and I are together and I have a potentially great job to focus on.

I ring Alex to let him know I'm on my way and then sit back and close my eyes. I can still feel the sea air on my face, still taste the wine that I drank while Mum and I sat on the beach and shared snippets of our lives. One thing I regret is moving so far away from my family: My dad is always working, so he was never around to miss, but Mum and I were always together and laughing. When I got into my teens, we were always sharing secrets and friends until she encouraged me to move away and have some independence.

I'm glad I did, and it led me to have the courage to travel with Amy when things got rough.

Part of me wonders though, what things would have been like if I'd moved back home when Luke and I broke up. When I pondered this out loud on the beach yesterday, Mum simply waved her hand and laughed.

"Darling, I love you and you're always welcome to come home. But your making your own home now, and I'm so proud of you for that" She gave me a cuddle and ordered another round.

I did seem to forge my own way while I wasn't looking: Life just seemed to happen and I don't feel like I had much control over it. As I finish my lunch, I make a pact with myself that I will appreciate things with Alex and put my all into this new job. The only way to get over my lost feeling is to embrace home and the family I've met along the way.

Sam

It's a quiet night at work, and I'm talking Nick through the new menu ideas as Ben walks through the doors. He smiles at Nick before reaching for me, but I lean out of the way, grabbing a cloth and heading to a few tables to clean up.

"Hey, what's wrong? "He asks, following me to a quiet corner of the bar.

"Oh, I don't know. I thought perhaps you'd have met up with Amy again rather than come here?" I spit out, not quite achieving the aloof mood I was hoping for.

"Amy? Why would I meet up with her?" He looks puzzled, and I grab my phone to show him the photo.

"Sam, I didn't meet her. We were both at the same place and she wanted to take a photo" He reaches for the phone with a frown.

"But she's your ex? " I look at him, my eyes wide and angry.

"Not an ex-girlfriend, just an ex fling. We were never together" He, again, has the good grace to look slightly ashamed.

"So she's a notch of your bed post? It seems she wants to stay there" I reply, wishing I could rise above this.

"Sam, we've talked about this. We both have pasts, but I don't see why that should get in the way of us" He grabs my hands and pulls me down to sit at the table.

"I know; I just don't like having it flaunted in my face. Especially when it's someone who I know, and who has a certain reputation" I sigh, knowing that I have no leg to stand on with this argument. I just don't like seeing my boyfriend in photos with his ex's.

"I'm sorry, I met Amy when we were both studying and we had a drunken night together. I barely remember it, but we'd remained friends and her friend must have taken that picture. Forgive me?" He begins to play with my fingers and then traces my lips into a smile with his thumb. I relent, his hands cooling away the anger that was rampant a few minutes ago. I kiss him, wondering how you're meant to protect your heart when you've already given it away.

Alex

I put the dirty plates in the sink and carry the bottle through to top up Ruby's wine glass.

"Thanks for dinner babe, it was delicious" She reaches up to kiss me, and I laugh as she pulls me down onto the sofa, somehow without spilling any wine.

"You're welcome. I wanted to mark the start of your new job and the first night we've had together for almost a week" I settle next to her, enjoying the heat of her body against mine.

"I know it's been a while, and Brighton was lovely. I did miss you though" She says as her fingers start to play with the skin on my stomach where my t-shirt has ridden up. I gasp quietly, liking that her touch still gives me goose bumps. As I look into her eyes, her smile fades.

"It's good to have you home, the bed was cold without you" I say, my voice gradually becoming lower as her hand does the same.

My hand meets hers before she reaches the buttons of my jeans. I want tonight to be special, and I want to take things slowly. I hold her hand and pull her along with me as we turn off the TV and walk through to the bedroom.

She looks up at me, her eyes as beautiful and warm as they were on the first night she spent in my bed. I undress her, still relishing the feeling of her skin touching mine as she starts to remove my own clothes. I want to look at her forever, but after a few nights without her, I feel that I might explode if I don't let the passion run free.

I take her in my arms, running my fingertips over her whole body as I lower us both onto the bed. It feels so good to have her home again, and I want her to know that.

Ruby

It's been almost a month since I took this job, and I'm exhausted.

I've been going to different gigs each week, which isn't really new to me, but I have to take notes now and make sure I take plenty of photos too. Sometimes Alex comes with me, but he works a lot of the time too so I either go alone or take Millie. She's never really followed much music, but she's happy to come along and dance to whatever I'm watching that night.

If I'm not out at gigs, I'm likely to be at home writing the reviews or watching films with Alex when we get a night together. It doesn't seem to matter that we're both so busy: Whenever we're both at home we still feel that same intensity, having days off where we do little else than enjoy each other. It's good to have someone who I know so well, but who somehow still gives me butterflies.

I'm at home now, finishing an article on a group called Band of Skulls that Millie and I saw last week. They're a new band from Southampton who are trying to get their name known locally in between supporting bigger bands nationally. They were really good, and I'm happily writing the last few lines as I start to feel a bit green.

I save the finished article before walking

through to the kitchen and checking the date on the microwave meal I ate an hour ago. It all looks fine, but my stomach doesn't agree.

I hear Alex's key in the front door as I finally retreat from the bathroom with what must be a pale face.

"Hey, you OK?" He asks, drawing me in for a hug.

"I don't know, I just felt ill all of a sudden" I shrug, suddenly holding my stomach again as I feel less than pleasant. I make a dash to the bathroom, leaving Alex looking confused and concerned.

Millie

I close the door behind the last child and survey the damage.

Today was the first workshop in my shop: Teaching children to make beaded bracelets. It was a lot of fun, and I managed to sell quite a few of the kits I'd put together for them too.

About ten kids turned up with their parents, eager to learn how to make the items that I'd displayed on the promotional pictures. They were so excited to learn the skills and a few of them even made jewellery for each other by the end of the hour session.

The shop looks like the aftermath of a break in, but I've had so much fun and made a few extra friends – As well as securing a number of repeat customers. The children were wandering around the shop, asking if they could learn to make other things. I could make this a weekly class and it would really help my sales.

I ring Sam with the news of a great day – It was her idea after all. She sounds a bit upset, so I tell her I'll stop by and see her at work after I cash up. I begin to clear away the beads and small tools that litter the table, wondering what happened to my best friend and resolving to buy her a thank you present – or at least a drink – after the great advice that may well be able to save my business.

Alex

I press the button to open the train doors and step out into Southampton station.

It's been a long day at work – someone rang in sick so we've been stretched to cover what is now becoming a 'lunch rush'. Sam's snack menu ideas were approved by head office so she made a deal with the local bakers to buy in some stock for a reduced price until she can put a plan into place for doing it ourselves. It's proving popular so far, but means that we'll need to recruit for a few more part timers.

I smile as I remember Ruby saying there are no gigs planned for tonight. As much as I like going out to watch live music with her, I much prefer nights at home. We're still enjoying that amazing honeymoon period of our relationship – Days and nights full of laughter, flirting and sex. There's something amazing about sleeping with someone you love after a few years of meaningless encounters. I'm still waiting for something to go wrong, while doing everything in my power to keep things working.

I let myself into the flat, my smile fading slightly as I see a glass of water and some painkillers lying on the coffee table. Ruby's been feeling unwell for a few days now, and I'm concerned that she's becoming overtired with all the work she's been doing. I'd hoped she'd feel better so we could spend some time together rather than her falling asleep on my lap as she has most nights this week.

I call out to her, taking a seat on the sofa as she opens the bathroom door. I can't quite read her expression, but as I get to my feet to greet her I see her bring a hand from behind her back. She's holding a small plastic thing, that I suddenly realise is a pregnancy test. I feel my smile before I can stop it, seeing her eyes fill up as she tries and fails to mirror my happy expression.

Sam

Today has been stressful to say the least.

We were a staff member short for the new and improved lunch time period, and Alex, Nick and I were rushed off our feet. This does have the silver lining of proving that my idea can be successful though, so we just need to get used to the extra custom it brings.

The worst part of the day came at mid-afternoon when I sat down for a quick break and checked my phone. I made the mistake of logging onto Facebook, which brought up another photo of Ben with Amy. It was an old photo of the two of them, obviously taken on a drunken night out. I looked at it for a while, wondering if that was the night that they spent together. It was pointless and petty – as Amy herself seems to be – but I sent Ben a text to ask why he was happy to be tagged in a photo where he was being kissed by an ex 'fling'. He was apologetic, though a bit tongue tied for an explanation, and promised to meet me from work to make it up to me. I've never been a jealous person, but I don't like the knowledge that some random girl is trying to get closer to my boyfriend when all they shared was a one night stand a few years ago.

"Penny for your thoughts" Millie says as she sits down at the bar. She's snuck in without me seeing.

I show her the photo, relieved as she sneers in the same way I did. I don't want to talk it through again, having gone through the whole thing in my head countless times in the last few hours. I pour her a glass of wine, and then look up to find Ben opening the door. I sigh, Millie following my gaze and giving my hand a quick squeeze.

"Sam, what time do you finish?" He asks, bending to kiss me with more passion than I respond with.

"In an hour, feel free to stay for a drink but I don't want to talk here" I say, moving to wipe the bar so I have something to do.

"OK, I've left a few of my housemates in a pub down the road. I'll be back before you close, I promise. I won't interrupt you and Millie" He gives Millie a quick smile before walking back out. I suddenly feel angry that I've finally let someone close enough to make me feel so vulnerable.

Millie and I talk as I begin to clear the tables – It's quiet tonight, with no entertainment planned, and that's quite nice after the busy day. When Millie finally finishes her second glass of wine and passes it to me to be cleaned, I see Ben stood outside and Nick nudges my arm.

"You go Sam, I'll finish up here" He winks at me and I smile with gratitude. Millie and I walk out together, though she drops back a bit as we reach my boyfriend.

"Hi" He says, kissing me again as I wish it didn't make me melt.

"Ben, I'm not really in the mood to talk but I'm getting tired of you being pictured everywhere with that bimbo" I say, pulling away and beginning to walk up the road.

"I know, but you have to believe that nothing happened since that night a few years ago. Amy's always taking photos and she must have taken a few when I was drunk. She wanted to stay friends, and I was having breakfast with my housemate when she appeared and wanted to say hi" He shrugs, sighing deeply as I finally turn back to him.

"OK, I believe you. But, why is she posting old photos now? Does she still like you?" I ask, feeling insecure and hating it.

"I don't know. She knew as well as I did at the time that it was just fun. She posts a lot of photos, so maybe she just found some old ones. I can ask her to stop" He says, looking into my eyes as we hear someone calling his name.

Just as I break my gaze from his smile, I realise that voice belongs to the last person I want to see.

"Amy? What do you want?" I can't help myself from smiling at the impatience in his voice.

"I just saw you and thought I'd say hi. We're heading to a house party if you want to come?" She flicks her perfect, sleek hair over a bare shoulder, looking coyly up at Ben.

"Amy, I'm going home with my girlfriend. My housemates are further up the hill if you want to catch them up" He takes my hand and kisses it.

"Fair enough, maybe another time?" She looks hopefully up at him through her long eyelashes. I've been silent until now, but I need to say my piece.

"Look, Amy is it? I'm sorry to be so blunt but you need to leave my boyfriend alone. I know you want to have fun, and some men might be up for that. I'm afraid Ben isn't available for your kind of slutty fun anymore, he's with me. Now let us go home and feel free to crawl back into whichever hole you came out of."

I keep hold of Ben's hand as I begin to march past Amy up the hill. I try not to stare at her shocked expression, almost as much as I try not to join Millie as she giggles behind me.

Ruby

I'm sat on the side of the bath, feeling my heart sink to my feet.

I've never taken a pregnancy test before, but something told me after the last few days that it was possible. I bought a test and then walked home in a daze, wondering what I'd tell Alex and what the hell we would do if it was positive.

We're happy and secure, but we've only been together for a few months. I have no idea what I'd do, what I'd want to do if that little blue line appears. I do want a family, but in a 'one day' kind of sense – Someday in the future when I'm grown up and feel capable of taking care of another person.

I'm not sure how Alex would feel, though I know that he partly ended his relationship with Kate due to a pregnancy scare. Granted, it was the fact that she lied about it rather than the pregnancy itself, but I don't think either of us would be ready for something this big when our relationship is so new.

My phone beeps to tell me that three minutes have passed. My heart suddenly leaps from my feet into my throat and it takes me a few moments to calm myself down enough to look at the stick.

Oh shit.

There's the line. Have I read the instructions

right? I pick up the packet to be sure, and then hear
Alex calling my name. I suppose my only option is
to tell him now, but what will his reaction be?

I open the bathroom door, holding the stick
behind my back to try and soothe my own sanity.
As I meet his eye, I catch my hand on my jeans
and pull it away, releasing the pregnancy test and
holding it out to him, not knowing how else to tell
him. My mouth has gone dry and I can't seem to
form words. His face lights up and he smiles down
at me. I breathe out a sigh of relief that he seems
happy, only to feel a wave of nausea and panic at
what I'm holding in my hand. I feel the prick of
tears behind my eyelids and try to mirror his smile,
but my mouth won't react so instead I take a deep
breath and fold into him as he pulls me in for a
hug.

2010: (3 Years Later)
Ruby

My mind is racing in what feels like a thousand directions, but I can't quite open my eyes.

I can hear Alex calling my name, but it feels like I'm underwater. As soon as the nurse started talking about blood types and paternity concerns, something in my head clicked and now I'm reeling from the flashes of almost memory.

There are only snippets, like the flashbacks you see on films, but they are all too real and disturbing and I can't let them in. Behind my eyelids I can see a face that once meant love and protection, but suddenly showed a violent streak and still now brings fear to my stomach. I force my eyes to open and rid myself of the image, and am confronted instead with the shocked face of my love.

"Ruby, are you ok?" Alex asks, his eyes full of concern, though there's a trace of something else underneath.

Anger? Disbelief? I can't quite be sure, but I blink and nod. He helps me up to sitting, then kisses my forehead and mutters something about getting some fresh air. He walks out of the room, and I'm left alone on the floor. I move onto a nearby chair and take a deep breath: I don't know how long I was out for but I have a feeling creeping like icy fingers up my back towards my neck, knowing that something is very wrong.

The door opens again and the nurse looks at me with worry and compassion. She holds out a glass of water and I take a sip. As she starts to talk to me in calming tones, I discover that I was unconscious for a matter of minutes, and that she'd like to have me checked over.

I start to protest, but the icy fingers feel like they're clawing at my throat. I don't understand what's going on, but within my thoughts I remember my baby.

"How's Mae?" I ask, looking to the nurse for some good news.

"She's doing much better. Luckily your friend was a match and so we got enough blood to help Mae. We'll keep her in for a few days to monitor her progress, but you can see her in a while if you like?" She smiles as I nod: the relief evident on my face.

"I do think that you should see a doctor after that though, you may have hit your head when you fell. Do you remember what happened?" She places a hand on my shoulder as I put my head in my hands.

I don't know if I can fathom what happened, or the repercussions of it. The idea that Alex might not be Mae's father is too much to contemplate.

Will Alex think I've been unfaithful? Should I

have told him about that night when I woke up alone and bruised in the alleyway? I remember getting home that morning, wanting to tell him but finding him drunk and asleep. There are so many confusing questions racing for space behind my eyes, and it's only when I open my eyes for relief that I see the nurse has been talking. I apologise and ask her to repeat her question, struggling to focus.

"I thought you might like to see a counsellor after the doctor has checked you over? It might help you deal with what's going on?" I smile weakly, wondering whether I can start to explain something when I don't understand it myself.

Alex

I fight my way through all the doors until I finally find an exit that leads to the open air.

I take some deep breaths as I walk past a few smokers – almost wishing I shared the same habit – and walk past the car park and onto the gardens beyond. Mae was born in this hospital, and the irony of being in the same place to find out that she's not actually mine is an evil blow.

As Ruby fainted upon hearing the news, we didn't get the chance to talk. Did she know all along? How could she not?

I can't quite rest on a single thought, they are all rushing around my brain and I'm almost running across the grass to try and keep up. I feel my legs start to burn with the effort, and make myself sit down in an attempt to make my thoughts still themselves as well.

It doesn't work, and as I reach for a few blades of grass to keep my hands busy I find myself craving the oblivion of alcohol. I don't want to get drunk, but my brain seems more comfortable with the idea of numbness than with emotional turmoil. I resolve that this is perhaps normal, but the events of the past twenty-four hours are anything but.

I should go back in and talk to Ruby, to find out what's going on and how we move forward from this. Can we move forward? Ever since we've been together – and more so since having Mae – I've felt like my life is complete and we can get through anything together. I never even thought that something could happen to blow it all apart, and now that it has I feel completely helpless and unprepared.

I glance down at my hands and see that I manage to have shredded grass and buttercups all over my shoes. I brush them off and stand up, walking over to a nearby bench. I can't see anyone else around, having run quite far from the hospital entrance. I run my hands through my hair to comb it out of my eyes, where it inevitably falls again within seconds.

I know I need to talk to Ruby and get some answers, but until I can form real thoughts I'll sit here and hope that the breeze will blow some of the cobwebs away.

Sam

After a few horrible hours of sitting in the waiting room without much news, I'm finally told I'm allowed to go and see my best friend.

Millie was kept in intensive care for a long time, and I knew that it had taken her a long time to wake up after the crash. I hadn't let myself imagine the conversation where the doctors told me that she wouldn't wake up, and now I can finally talk to her and see how she is.

I walk through with the nurse to a department on a separate floor from the paediatric ward where we've been sat for what feels like days. As we walk, the nurse – she's told me her name several times but there's too much in my head for it to stick – explains that Millie is recovering well but that her memory of the incident is sketchy so far and that I must try to keep her calm while I'm with her.

As I push the door open, I see that Millie is awake, but looks exhausted. I almost run towards her, leaning over for the closest thing we can get to a hug.

"Millie, how are you?" I ask, worried by how pale she looks.

"I'll live, so I'm told" She smiles warmly, holding the hand that I offer as I sit down on the edge of the bed.

"Do you remember anything?" I look into her eyes, but there is only frustration and fatigue staring back at me. The nurse slips from the room, telling me she'll be at the reception desk if we need anything.

"The last thing I remember is being in the car with you and Mae . . . We had to go back for that toy. What happened, Sam? Is Mae ok?" Millie's eyes grow wide as she looks to me for assurance.

"Mae is recovering; she's doing well and should be discharged soon. Ben was following us and there was a collision with another car. Alex said that there were only two cars when they found us though, so it looks like Ben drove off" As I talk, relieved that my own memory is improved, Millie's expression moves from relief to disbelief.

"Ben just left? Was the crash his fault? We should tell the police" She tries to sit up, but winces as her speech moves too fast for her recovering head. I stroke her arm, trying to calm her down.

"It seems like he just left, but Alex was told that the crash was caused by the third car. The thing is, that driver was admitted to hospital along with us and she seems to have fallen into a coma" I watch Millie frown, trying to take in this new information. I don't want to tell her anymore, but I can't keep it from her.

"Millie, there's something else. The third

driver wasn't a random stranger. Do you remember Kate?" Millie's frown deepens upon hearing a name from years ago and she looks at me.

"Alex's ex-girlfriend Kate?" She whispers, the shock showing in her eyes.

Ruby

I've been looking everywhere for Alex.

I still can't quite get my head to process the information from the hospital, but I think that talking to him will help me to clarify things. Also, I'm a bit scared that he might have left us. I shrug this thought off, knowing in my heart that even if he thought I'd been unfaithful, he wouldn't leave Mae without the assurance that she was fully recovered.

I open the doors onto the main entrance and scan the gardens. Perhaps he went for a walk? I begin to amble across the grass, and after a while I can see the outline of someone sitting on a bench on the outskirts of the grounds. It takes me a while to reach him, and he doesn't hear me approach – Too caught up in his thoughts. I'm not sure how to start the conversation, so I decide to gently play with his hair by means of a greeting. He flinches slightly, before recognising my touch and turning his head.

"Can we talk?" I ask warily.

"I think it's about time, given what I've just found out" He doesn't quite smile, but gestures to the space on the bench beside him.

"Alex, there's something I should have told you a long time ago. It's not what you're thinking I'm sure, but I need to be honest" I take a seat and face him, his face open and ready for an explanation.

"Do you remember the day that I first got offered the music reviewing job? Amy and I went out to celebrate that night?" He nods and I take his hand as I continue.

"Well, Luke had arrived to help Millie with the craft shop. They were at the same pub, although we hadn't arranged to meet. I went outside to ring you, and then I found Luke drunk in the alleyway" I pause to take a deep breath, my hands beginning to shake where they rest in his as I delve deeper into what I think I remember.

"Please, Ruby, tell me you didn't sleep with him?" His voice cracks, his hands pulling away from mine.

"No, I'd never do that to you!" I'm shocked at his assumption, though in the current situation it's only logical. I see him sigh deeply.

"I'm sorry, but I just found out that Mae isn't mine and really, I'm a bit lost for words. Just be honest with me"

"I remember waking up later, in the alleyway, with no one around. I had no idea what had happened, though I had a few bruises and I felt . . . sore. It's still a blur to look back on, but I just wanted to get home to you. I got the train back and . . . you were passed out on the sofa. The next day I went to Brighton and I talked to mum. She was worried that I was frustrated and couldn't remember anything. I know Luke tried to kiss me and I pushed him away and fell, but that's all. I wanted to forget it and focus on us, and a month later we got pregnant" I pause again, watching as Alex remembers my reluctance to have the baby.

"I didn't know what had happened, and I've only ever been with you and Luke. I've never been unfaithful to you Alex, but I think that Luke might have . . . "I find myself unable to finish the sentence as my own voice cracks and a tear escapes from the corner of my eye.

"Do you think he raped you?" Alex asks, his hand gripping mine and I see his face drain of colour as he says the word.

"Alex, I don't know. I've never let myself think about that night and I never questioned that Mae was yours. When the nurse told us that she wasn't, something about that night flashed into my head. .. I saw Luke's face and it was like my brain couldn't process it. I still don't really know what happened, and I'm not sure I want to, but I need you to believe that I didn't betray you" I stop, having managed to get the last few sentences out through deep sobs.

At some point, Alex must have knelt down in front of me because he's looking deeply into my eyes whilst holding my hands.

"Ruby I love you. I've been out here trying to

work out what I'd do if you admitted to sleeping with someone else. I was trying to imagine it, but we've always been so happy that I couldn't get to grips with the idea" He pauses to kiss my hand and then sits back down beside me.

"Do you think that you might remember fully what happened if you tried?" He ventures, playing with a hole in my jeans.

"I don't know; I've tried so hard to forget about it. The nurse offered to put me in contact with a counsellor, but how do you remember things from when you were unconscious?" I look down at my hands, now in fists on my thighs.

"Perhaps you need to confront Luke directly, or I should?" Alex places his hand over mine, facing me.

"I'm not sure I can see him again Alex, especially not if we're right" I move to stand, but Alex holds my hands tight.

"Ruby, this won't change anything with us. I'm not going anywhere. Regardless of DNA, Mae's always been my daughter and I won't give that up. I won't give us up. But if Luke has hurt you- "He stands up, and I suddenly realise how angry this has made him.

"He hasn't hurt me if I don't remember it. If you want to find out, that's fine, but I don't want to see him. I know that Millie is still in contact with him for the business, so you could ask her for his number?" I stand up with him, realising how bizarre this situation is.

"OK, I'll talk to her. Could we keep this between us though? I don't want people to think that I'm not Mae's dad" He asks, leaning down to embrace me. I kiss him, bringing his hands to my hips and taking comfort from the contact.

"Alex, no matter what you find out, you're Mae's dad. You always have been. We both know that, and I won't have some random blood type telling us otherwise" I kiss him again, wishing that we could kiss away the potential truth.

Millie

I'm not sure what drugs they've put me on, but ever since I woke up I've been struggling to make sense of anything.

I lie in my bed, drifting in and out of sleep, and trying to be nice to the nurses that come to do the tests. They seem happy with me and I hear phrases like 'making progress' and 'out of the woods' but I'm still here, apparently waiting to be taken off the drugs so that I can go home.

During one of my less lucid moments, I see Alex walk through the door and sit tentatively on the seat beside my bed. He looks exhausted, and slightly upset, but he's quiet as he waits for me to speak.

"Hi" I say, unable to offer more by way of conversation.

"Hey, how are you feeling?" He asks, a strange sentence from someone who looks like he's been through hell.

"Honestly? I feel sedated" I reply with a tired smile.

"That sounds good to me" Alex closes his eyes, sighing deeply.

"How are you? Sam said that Mae's doing well. I'm so sorry for what happened" I start, trying to sit up but it takes too much energy. Alex leans forward and puts his hand on my shoulder, gently pushing me back down.

"I'm OK, but it's been a long few days. I wondered if I could ask you a favour without any questions asked" He takes a deep breath and then catches my eye.

I look into his eyes, feeling like I can see into him, and whatever he's going through is tearing him apart. I want to help him, this man that I've known for years and have seen grow from a broken shell of a friend into an established, loving father. I sit and nod, listening to his request and I know that I need to respect whatever it is that he needs, if only as an apology for what I let happen to Mae.

Sam

Now that I know Millie's recovering, I've found space in my head to remember the nurse's name.

Nancy – A traditional, dependable name for a lovely woman – found me in the waiting room of Millie's ward to tell me that Kate has regained consciousness but is still in intensive care. I walk through to tell Millie and find Alex with her. I feel torn but have to tell him what's happening: I'm surprised but relieved that he wants to come with me to the ICU.

As we walk there, I glance at Alex and see how much the last few days has taken out of him. I can't imagine what he's going through, waiting for his daughter to get better, but we've always had quite an open friendship so I hope he might let me in. I can't quite find the words to ask how he is, but as soon as we walk into Kate's room a shadow passes over his face as if he's seen a ghost and I know my window of opportunity is gone for now.

"Alex?" Her voice is croaky, almost a whisper, but she reaches her hand out to him. Alex looks frozen to the spot, so I walk towards the girl that broke his heart.

"Kate, how are you?" I ask, taking her hand as she looks at me blankly, perhaps wondering who I am. It suddenly occurs to me that she may not remember me, but it doesn't seem the time for introductions.

She shrugs with a sigh, and I drop her hand gently back onto the bed.

"Kate" Alex suddenly awakens from his trance and joins me by the side of the bed, refusing to touch her but transfixed by her eyes all of a sudden.

"What happened?" She asks, locking eyes with him.

"You crashed into a car that had two of my friends and my daughter inside" Alex says, though he stumbles over the sentence.

"Your daughter? I didn't think you wanted children" Kate's voice is still little more than a whisper, but the sorrow in her words is clear.

"I just didn't want them with you" He says, before realising what he's said and stepping backwards.

"I shouldn't have come, but you'd best hope that my child is OK" With that he slips from the room, and I turn back to Kate, wondering why I'm sitting here with a woman that I never really knew.

"Don't worry about him, he's had a tough few days" I explain, realising how ironic a sentence that is to say to someone in Intensive Care.

"Haven't we all?" Kate replies, reading my mind.

"I know, and I hope you get better soon. I'd better go and check on Alex. Take care" I say with a quick smile, making my way back to Millie's ward in the hope of finding Alex.

Alex

This is something I never saw myself doing.

After talking to Millie, I asked Sam for Luke's address and now find myself on the train on the way to Manchester. I have no idea what I'll say when I see him, but I need to know that Ruby is telling the truth.

The idea that I'd rather my girlfriend was attacked if the alternative is that she was unfaithful must say horrible things about me, but either way I need to hear Luke tell me what happened that night. I get off the train and follow the instructions from my phone's sat-nav app until I arrive at the address that Sam found online for Ruby's ex-boyfriend. I knock on the door; half expecting for a stranger to answer, but the face that I envied a lifetime ago appears instead.

"Alex?" He is understandably wary.

"Luke, I'm sorry to disturb you. I just wanted to talk if you have a moment?" I take a breath, unsure suddenly whether I actually want my questions answered.

"OK, come in" He says, ushering me inside and upstairs. I suddenly realise that it's Luke's parent's house and this makes me feel like I have the upper hand, though in a vulnerable way. I have a flat and a child, though that may be blown out of the water in the next few minutes. We sit down on a small sofa in his room, and I am overcome with the feeling that I don't want to do this. I take a deep breath, knowing that this is not for me, but for my family.

It's been a long time since I saw him, but other than having slightly longer hair dangling into his face he looks the same. He always looked physically intimidating, being quite tall and broad in contrast to my thin frame. Though I was never scared of him in the past, spending several years seeing him almost as a brother, there's now an edge of aloofness to him that makes me feel uneasy.

"Luke, I'm not sure how to say this, so I'll just go ahead and say it. You know that Ruby and I have been together for a few years now, and we actually have a daughter – Mae. Mae was in a car accident a few days ago and needed some blood, so we both donated. The thing is . . . They tested the blood and we found out that I'm not Mae's biological father" I put the emphasis on biological, and manage to keep my voice even until I reach the next sentence.

"Ruby told me about that night when she saw you and you tried to kiss her. I don't know what happened, because Ruby passed out and doesn't remember, but I need to know if you . . . did anything that night that I should know about?" I take a breath, not knowing how else to word that without using the word rape. I can't speak that word out loud again, in case it makes me physically sick.

"Let me get this straight. You've come to my parent's house to ask if I raped my ex-girlfriend two years ago?" The ease with which he says that sentence makes my skin crawl.

I can see from his stance that he's suddenly trying to restrain himself, his hand clenched in a fist on the arm of the sofa, and I wish I'd had the presence of mind to think this trip through before getting on the train.

"Basically, yes" I say, unsure where this conversation will lead.

"You need to get out" Luke almost whispers the words as he stands up, walking downstairs without looking to see if I'm following. Once I finally catch up with him and we reach the front door, he opens it before a slight sneer appears on his face.

"You know, you might want to ask Ruby again what happened that night" I look up to see him grinning, though his face is ashen.

"What?" I ask, wanting to put an end to my curiosity. Upstairs, he looked as if he was moments from putting my face through a wall but he now seems to have regained control and be almost enjoying having me on the back foot. The fact that he's grinning after what I asked him brings my own hands into fists, looking in disgust at this man that used to be my friend.

"I've never forced myself on anyone, but we both know how friendly Ruby can get after-"He doesn't finish the sentence because I hit him, sending him sprawling against the doorframe.

I don't even look back as I walk away, knowing I never should have come here. I don't know what I expected, but I never fully expected an honest answer from the man that had once hit the woman I love.

Sam

Millie has been told that she could be discharged tomorrow.

We celebrate with a walk around the grounds, and come across Nancy, the kind nurse – having a sneaky cigarette on a break. Her eyes light up when she sees us, though they are watery and make me anxious somehow.

"Girls, I hoped I'd run into you before you went home" She says, drawing us nearer as she waves goodbye to a fellow nurse that walks back towards the entrance.

"You visited Kate Hughes the other day?" Nancy looks to me for recognition.

"Well, I'm sorry to tell you this but she never woke up this morning. It seems that she may have passed in her sleep last night . . . She had some internal bleeding" She searches my eyes, but only finds a twinge of sadness.

"Nancy, that's a real shame. Thanks for letting us know, but we're still waiting for news on Mae. Are Kate's family coming to be with her?" I smile as Nancy nods, and thank her again as we make our way back inside to check on Mae's progress.

I'm left wondering whether I should feel more affected by Kate's death, but I have friends and a child to think about. Kate was partly to blame for the crash, though Ben seems to have escaped without any finger pointing. I take a deep breath, hoping that he gets his comeuppance at some point.

Ruby

I sit in an uncomfortable chair next to my daughter's bed.

The nurses are full of good news, but we are yet to actually see Mae wake up. We are told that this is normal for such a small child, but it hurts regardless.

The other thing that hurts is that Alex left to go and talk to Luke, and hasn't come back yet. I let him go, and he would argue that I told him to go, but I didn't think that he would need to. I have no real recollection of that night, but maybe he doesn't believe that. Perhaps he thinks that I got drunk and made a mistake that I'm still unwilling to own up to. Should I not be upset that the man I love doesn't believe me when I tell him I was attacked?

Perhaps that's the problem, that I can't prove the attack? I've never been one to cry wolf, so thought that it was best to try and forget rather than accuse the one person that I never wanted to see again. The idea that the man I'd chosen to share my life with would be affected by that night never even factored into my thoughts, and my Mum had soothed away the doubts I'd had. Naive perhaps, but I'd hoped that after the issues I had with Luke's violence in the past, that I could chalk this up to a random drunken night out and focus on the

better things in life.
    Apparently not.

Alex

I wish I could say I wasn't confused.

I've been sat on the same seat on this train for over two hours, but I'm yet to find clarity. I love Ruby, and I would trust her with my life, but can I trust what she doesn't remember? That's one hell of a leap of faith for anyone, and given that Mae is currently yet to recover in a hospital bed, I'm not sure what I have left in terms of faith.

I hear the announcement for Southampton Central station and make my way towards the doors. I want to believe my girlfriend, but something about what Luke said has stayed with me. I hate that he's manipulated me enough to doubt Ruby, but she was once drunk enough to kiss me when she was with him.

We need to talk this through, and that thought makes me anxious in itself. Will she admit something, or will she be angry that I have questioned her? There's only one way to find out.

I walk the short distance between the station and the flat, feeling relief and disappointment in the same breath as I see that there's no sign of Ruby.

As I approach the door though, I realise there is someone standing outside. A strange sense of recognition mixes with dread as the face of Kate's sister, Alison, comes into full view. My mind flicks back to seeing Kate in a hospital bed, pale and swollen, and before I can think past that Alison grabs hold of my jacket and starts flailing.

"Are you happy now?! She's dead! She's . . . gone" I stand there saying nothing, merely watching Ali as she loses hold of me and keels over on the step that leads from the pavement to our front door.

She looks up at me from her crouched position, her long limbs giving her the look of an injured stick insect. She was always a bit too thin; taller than Kate and made to look quite severe by the way she wore her dark blonde hair so short. It's been a while since I saw her last – She hadn't arrived at the hospital when I was taken to see Kate – and her hair is now almost to her shoulders, though it's looking unkempt as if to mirror her emotional state.

After a few seconds of staring at her in a heap on my doorstep, my mind seems to catch up with the situation and I finally respond.

"Kate's dead?!" I ask, wondering how I should feel.

"She didn't wake up this morning . . . She's gone" Ali tries to speak through the tears but struggles and sobs.

I reach out my hand to steady her and help her up, but she bats it away and all I can do is open the door and coax her inside gently: Neither of wants to be fighting on the pavement.

"I talked to her, she was awake . . . "I lead Ali through our front door, trying to clear my head enough to make sense of time. Was it really just yesterday that I was talking to Kate?

"Yeah, well, they said that she'd had some internal bleeding from her injuries, she was sleeping and now she's . . . "Ali's face begins to crumble again so I let her fall onto the sofa as I fetch her a glass of water.

"Where's your girlfriend?" I hear her sneer from the tiny kitchen.

"She's at the hospital with our daughter" I hear my voice catch and clear my throat. Kate's sister isn't someone who I want to appear vulnerable in front of.

I hand Alison the glass, seeing realisation dawn on her face as she accepts that her family wasn't the only one affected by what had happened.

"Didn't you break up with my sister because you didn't want a family?" Is all she says, and my head snaps to meet her eye line.

"I'm not discussing this with you" I say, gesturing for her to drink.

"Oh no, sorry, it was because you found someone else, I forgot" She retorts, sitting back to see if I rise to the bait. I sigh and look her straight in the eye.

"Ali, I understand you're upset. I'm sorry . . . I never wanted Kate to get hurt back then. I saw her yesterday; she was talking to me. I had no idea she . . . "I can't quite bring myself to finish the sentence.

"You talked to her?" Alison almost spits out the question, as if it tastes poisonous on her tongue. All I can do is nod.

"What did you say to her? Did you upset her?!" Her voice is rising, and I can see the tears in her eyes.

I try not to let the wave of shame that I feel show on my face, but as I think back to the last words I said to Kate I know they're likely to haunt me. It doesn't seem fair to add to Ali's anger and hurt, so I take a deep breath and shake my head.

"You expect me to believe that you said 'get well soon'?" She looks at me, and it's as if she sees right through me.

"I told her I had a daughter who had been in the car, and then I left" I stand up to get another glass for myself so I can avoid meeting her gaze.

"So she knew you'd got a family now, after not wanting children with her" She looks me up and down with disgust, and I focus on keeping my voice steady and calm.

"Will you stop pretending you don't know how things ended between us?" I maintain eye contact until she looks away, a tear snaking its way down her cheek.

"Do you think I care how this makes you feel Alex? My sister's dead. I'm sorry if that makes you feel guilty or ashamed or whatever the hell you feel but I don't care . . . Since Kate came home, she's been a wreck, and then she comes back here to get some closure from you and she ends up seeing you and the girl you left her for getting engaged, before getting in her car and getting killed. Now, you tell me how that's fair when you walk away and enjoy your new life?!" She stops finally, panting slightly.

"What? How did she know I was going to propose?" I try to think back but my mind won't clear.

"She sent me a text when she saw you in the restaurant; she was so upset that she left to drive home before the reunion" Ali's words finally break through and I put my head in my hands.

Finally seeing a reaction as she'd hoped for, Ali stands up. She still seems unstable on her feet, but manages to stumble across to the door before holding onto the handle and turning back to deliver the final blow.

"Kate never would have come back had she not needed to get over you, remember that. Remember what you did to her" Somehow she says her piece before starting to sob again, slamming the door behind her and leaving me to choke on the words that hang in the silence.

I collapse onto the sofa, but suddenly feel restless and so start pacing around the tiny lounge in an attempt to clear my head. My mind can't process the fact that Kate's gone – I'd not seen her for a long time, but the idea that she was dead after I'd spent almost a decade of my life loving her was too much to fathom.

I shake my head roughly, but rather than clearing the clouds away, the motion seems to mix my thoughts up further and somehow I find myself stood in the kitchen, trying not to look up at the blue storage box that sits on top of the highest cupboard. After Ruby moved in, we had bought some extra boxes to store random kitchen things that we hardly used, and this is the only one out of her reach: For that reason, I put some of my old gadgets in there as well as a bottle of vodka that I didn't want to waste but didn't want her to see.

That was a few years ago now, and I'm almost proud to think that this is the first time I've felt myself drawn to it. I don't want to drink it, but the idea of escaping the mess of thoughts running round my head is comforting.

I stand there for a long time, even ignoring an incessant buzzing in my pocket, willing myself to walk away, challenging myself to be stronger than I know I actually am.

Ruby

I sigh deeply and try to stop myself from getting angry.

Alex is ignoring my calls, apparently not concerned that I'm sat here with potential news of Mae's condition. It rang for some time before his voicemail message kicked in, so I know he's got reception.

I scroll through my phone contacts, wondering who else I can ring to bring some extra clothes for my daughter: I don't want to leave her, and Mum's on her way but I could really do with her support rather than her running errands for us. I smile as Sam's number flashes up on the display, making my decision for me.

"Hi" I answer.

"Wow that was quick!" She giggles, the familiarity of her voice filling me with relief already.

"I was actually looking through my phone to find someone to do me a favour . . . What are you up to?" I hold my breath, hoping she's free.

"I was sat here wondering how you and Mae are doing. What do you need?" She replies, listening while I remind where the spare key is hidden.

She assures me that she'll be at the hospital within the hour, so I settle back into the uncomfortable green chair and watch Mae sleep.

Sam

I balance gingerly on my tiptoes, frustrated that I can feel the spare key on top of the soft stone block above the door frame, but I'm struggling to reach it. I'm stood on the top step, and can't see anything else to stand on. I decide the best I can do is to jump to get the keys and risk getting a face full of stone.

After two tries, I manage to brush the key off the block and it drops with a satisfying clink at my feet. I finally let myself in, wondering if I should have knocked first in case Alex is in.

I shout a quick greeting into the flat that is met with silence, so I go straight into Mae's room to gather the extra clothes that Ruby asked for. I locate a holdall in the tiny wardrobe that I add different things to, thinking what else might be needed.

When I walk back through to the lounge, I spot Alex's keys on the table – they have his work keys on a separate ring, as well as a photo of Ruby and Mae that he took and then paraded around at work after she was born – and frown. Why would he leave his keys at home if he'd gone out? I shout out to him again, but there's no answer.

I pick the holdall back up, but drop it suddenly onto the sofa as I hear a small groan coming from the kitchen. I run in to see Alex's body limp and unmoving on the floor, the broken shards of a bottle lying around him like the cracking ice of a frozen pond. I feel my chest rise in a silent gasp as I stop my feet just before they reach the broken glass, my eyes scanning the debris before alighting on the cause... the body of the bottle remains intact further from the mess, a familiar vodka label lazily meandering around on the floor, as if playing Spin the Bottle by itself.

Alex

I can hear someone talking, but it's as if I'm underwater.

All I remember is standing in the kitchen, looking up at the storage box and making a deal in my head that if I poured the alcohol into the sink, my daughter would get better. I reached up to pull the box down and as I lifted the bottle from inside it, I suddenly felt faint.

Now I can hear a familiar voice that I can't place calling my name, and I somehow manage to peel my eyelids apart to look up through the blurred picture that is my kitchen and locate Sam's petrified face.

"What the hell happened? Did you drink the whole bottle?" She screams at me, crouching down by my shoulder.

"No, I . . . "My voice fades, as I try to pull together all of my strength to set the story straight.

"Alex, get up! I thought you were past all this. Your family needs you and all you do is come home and drink until you pass out?!" She demands as she tries to coerce me up to sitting.

I feel like I've shakily swam up to the surface as I sit, and I take a few deep breaths before placing my head in my hands to steady my thoughts.

"I didn't drink" I say, though my thoughts are

so hazy I can't be sure I said it aloud.

"So, I find you passed out, in a puddle of vodka and broken glass, and you have another explanation?!" She looks at me, a pained and stern expression on her face.

"I . . . I didn't drink" I repeat, unsure of what else to say.

"Well, come on; let's get you back to the hospital. Ruby had asked me to pick up some things for Mae, and I think someone should check you over" She says, sighing deeply and shaking her head in a way so I know that she doesn't believe me.

Ruby

I have no idea what to do or how to solve the situation we've found ourselves in, so when my Mum rings I ask her to meet me at the hospital.

She already knew about the crash, but I'd left the other details out of the story so far. I had hoped that Alex and I could solve this alone, and he'd been clear that he wanted no one else to question the paternity of our child. I'd agreed to start with, understanding how he must feel having been blind sighted with this news. Things were slightly different now that Alex doubted me though, and I needed Mum to soothe and calm me as she had done in Brighton, and countless other times besides.

I sit with Mae, who is finally awake but woozy, and contemplate what might happen if Alex can't trust me. I had never thought that in a question of my fidelity or an attack, he would prefer to think that I'd betrayed him. I suppose because there's no proof, I should have expected that he might be confused, but to actually take Luke's side over mine is something that surprised and hurt me deeply.

My mum pops her head through the door with a sympathetic smile and, when she sees I'm alone, walks through to give me the warmest hug I've had since I've been at the seaside. Just to see her face takes me back to the safe place where we used to watch films together on the sofa under blankets when Dad went off on another business trip. I suddenly wonder whether she shares the same memories when she sees me, but I suppose that most people feel that about their mother. Something in her expression makes me blink back the tears that have built up this week. She sees this and pulls me back into her embrace. I don't want to cry, but I can't pretend with her, and I start to sob onto her shoulder.

"Let it out, Ruby. It's going to be OK" is all she says, stroking my back as I let go of all of the stress and the upset.

Part of me wishes that I could crawl into a cocoon of my childhood with just my Mum to keep me sane. The relief of Mae's recovery has lifted my spirits, but knowing that Alex and I have a struggle ahead of us is draining to say the least. I sink down into my chair as Mum collects another from the stack in the corner. I find that I can't compose myself, and instead end up taking deep, ragged breaths in an effort to calm my crying. Mum takes my hand and squeezes it, that small action alone giving me much needed life line to hold onto.

Suddenly, there's a quiet knock at the door followed by a hand swinging Mae's pink holdall and Sam's face in a pained smile.

"Thank you so much!" I say, taking the bag and placing it in the corner next to my chair. I gesture to the seat on the other side of the bed.

"Do you need to rush off?" I ask.

"Well, not really. I didn't come alone though; can I have a word?" The pained expression is etched on her face so I glance at mum who waves us into the corridor.

I follow Sam outside and close the door, wondering what else could have happened.

"Ruby, I found Alex when I went to pick up the clothes. He was passed out in the kitchen with a bottle of vodka smashed around him" My eyes grow wide as she explains.

"He said he wasn't drinking, but I don't know what to believe. I brought him here to get checked over so we'll know what happened soon" She says with a knowing look.

I've been so worried about Alex blaming me for things that it hadn't occurred to me he could have slipped back into dealing with problems the way he had in the past.

"I asked the doctor to come and find you as the next of kin when he's discharged Alex. Unless you'd rather I waited and took him home?" She asks, but I shake my head.

"I won't pretend I'm not disappointed, but it's my problem not yours. Thank you" I reply, giving Sam a brief hug before she kisses my cheek and retreats back down the corridor.

Millie

Sam opens the door, and I sigh with relief at finally being back at home.

The doctors finally released me this morning on the promise that Sam would take care of me and I would report back to them if I noticed any extra aches or pains.

"Can I get you a cup of tea?" Sam asks, but I just smile and know it was rhetorical.

I walk through to the lounge, letting my bags fall onto the small armchair while I fold myself gently onto the sofa: It's hard to get comfortable when you have a few bruised ribs and are recovering from a mild concussion, along with a smattering of bumps and bruises. The nurses assured me that none of the injuries should need much more than a few days' rest, but resting is difficult when you can't find a position in which to do so. I prop myself precariously among cushions, flashing Sam a pained smile as she walks through and places my favourite mug – blue and white stripes with a picture of a smiling monkey across the middle, that she once bought me from a seaside trip with Ben – on the table in front of me.

"How are you feeling?" She asks, wincing when she sees me move slightly and grimace at the pain in my lower chest.

"Sore, but I'll live. It's such a shame about

Kate" I reply, and we both grow silent. For all the time that we knew she was Alex's girlfriend, we'd only met her a handful of times. Yet, it feels odd that she's died.

"Is there any news on Mae?" I ask, keen to change the subject.

"Ruby said she was awake but woozy. It sounds like she's out of the woods" Sam gives me a small shrug and a relieved smile.

"I'm so glad she's OK. I feel so guilty about what happened" I reply.

"It's not your fault, Millie. Ben was chasing us. Perhaps we should have pulled over-"I hold out my hand to cut her off. What – ifs aren't going to help any of us now.

"Do you think Alex blames us?" Sam asks quietly, her wide eyes locking on mine.

"Not really, I just think we've all had a tough time and no one knows who to blame" I reply, shifting forward to reach my drink and take a small sip of the milky, sweet liquid.

"Did you mention anything about Ben at the hospital?" Her face suddenly pales as she looks at me.

"No Sam, I didn't. It's not my place to tell anyone about him but I think you should. It wasn't just a bump; his actions have killed someone. I know the police put the blame on Kate, but that's because they don't know about Ben. What if it was his fault and he gets away with that on top of everything else?!" I stop, forcing myself to stay still and take a deep breath.

I hadn't meant to rant, but this whole last week has been a tough one for Sam and I don't think she's thinking straight. She hasn't mentioned Ben since the crash, and I think she's been trying to forget him. Usually that would be a good thing, but not when he's to blame for someone's death?

"I'm sorry; I didn't mean to raise my voice. I just think that Ben should be accountable for what happened, don't you?" I meet her eyes, seeing the hint of a tear escaping from her almond shaped eyes. She blinks quickly, a hand reaching clumsily to brush her short dark hair over her cheek.

Alex

It took a while, but a nurse has finally cleared me as healthy.

Apparently, Sam had asked for me to be escorted to Mae's room, which she explained to me isn't normal procedure but as it was only a few corridors away she was happy to oblige.

Nurse Hopkins strides purposefully through the doors to the paediatric unit with me in tow and I spot Joy, Ruby's mum, talking on her phone. She looks up impatiently and I see her frown as she alights on my face. She opens Mae's door and beckons to Ruby who storms out of the room and into my field of vision. She stops a few feet from the nurse and looks at me with tired contempt.

"Well, I hope you're feeling better? I know its stressful Alex, but did you not think you might be needed here, or even want to be here to sit with me by Mae's side instead of going home to blot it all out with a bottle of vodka? I don't even know . . . "She runs out of steam at that point or perhaps sees Nurse Hopkins expression and is cut short.

Either way, she seems to ignore the look of disappointment on my face as I realise she was quick to believe the worst.

"Miss Taylor? Am I right in thinking that ~~your~~ you are Alex's next of kin?" The nurse asks, and Ruby nods dumbly.

"I'm afraid that Alex was brought to us after suffering from an intense case of shock. It seems he'd fainted whilst holding a glass bottle. There were no lasting injuries thankfully, just a few minor cuts on his hands. He'll need to take things a bit easily though for a few days" I see Ruby's confusion as her eyes move from me to the nurse, unsure what to say.

"We did take some blood tests as procedure, but there was nothing to worry about, and" the nurse clears her throat, slightly embarrassed at the scene unfolding before her, "there was no alcohol in his system"

I watch Ruby process this information, wishing that I could rewind the last few minutes and see her emerge from Mae's room concerned and relieved to see me. I thank the nurse, and before Ruby can find her voice I sneak through to catch a glimpse of my daughter. Mae's asleep, but there's colour in her cheeks and there's an empty yoghurt pot on the table next to her bed.

"She woke up this morning, they think she'll be home in a day or two when they've done a few more tests" Ruby says, refusing to meet my gaze but her tone is hopeful.

"That's great. Can you let me know when she's given the all clear? I'll make sure everything's ready at home" I offer her a small smile, but step away as she moves towards me.

I retreat back into the corridor, edging past Joy who is luckily still engrossed in a phone conversation. I've spent more time in this hospital than in my own home in the last few days, and I see why so many people hate hospitals.

Ruby

After Alex left, I've not been able to stop pacing around Mae's room – If you can call it pacing when the room is barely big enough to contain its cot and two chairs. Mum finally tells me to go home and have a shower. Mae's not long drifted off to sleep and I can be back in just over an hour so I accept a cuddle and rush off to wash away the smell of desperation that I'd almost come to accept as a new perfume.

I let myself into the flat, feeling a nasty sense of anxiety at what I might find.

Alex and I have had a few intense discussions recently, and the way he looked at me when he left the hospital scared me. I find him sat on the sofa, flicking through TV channels with what seems like sarcastic contempt for the programmes. It makes me smile, but his eyes find mine and take my smile away.

"How's Mae?" He asks, taking my hand cautiously and playing with my fingers,

"She's doing well. The doctors want to release her tomorrow" I reply, enjoying the feel of his hands.

Maybe I know him too well, but something about Alex's body language tells me that he's about to break my heart. I take a deep breath before I face him.

"I'm sorry for assuming you'd been drinking. Are you OK?" I say, unsure how else to start the conversation.

"Not really" He says as he sighs deeply and looks into my eyes.

"When you got into the ambulance with Mae, I recognised the other car. Kate was involved in the accident" He pauses as I gasp, but his gaze quietens me as I realise he has more to say.

"I went with Sam to see her, but soon after that she died. On the way back from seeing Luke, Kate's sister came to find me and she was really upset and angry. She told me that Kate had never got over me and that I was the reason she'd come back . . . Somehow Kate had been at the same restaurant the night of the crash . . . "He stops to clear his throat, and I see his face cloud over as if deciding whether to continue. I stay silent, willing him to carry on.

"Ruby, I'd planned to propose to you that night, and Kate must have been watching us . . . I hid the ring box under a napkin and somehow she saw it . . . I don't really know how . . . Ali said she left the restaurant upset, and then she ended up crashing into Sam's car. Ali said she blamed me for her sister's death and then stormed out. I knew I had one bottle of vodka in the flat, but I poured it away and somehow fainted. That's when Sam found me . . ." His speech tails off, and I sit back, trying to take it all in.

"Ruby, I don't want you to doubt that I want to be with you and Mae. I just feel so overwhelmed after the last week that I need some time on my own to figure things out" I pause, looking into her eyes.

"So, what are you saying? You want to move out?" I ask, feeling winded by his words.

"I can just go and stay at Millie's for a few days while you and your mum get Mae settled "He tries to hold my hand but I yank it away.

"I'll come back to see Mae tomorrow, will you let me know when your back?" He asks gently, but I avoid his eye line as I stand up.

I wipe a tear from my cheek in the same moment that Alex's ragged breathing betrays his own tears. I don't know how we made it all the way to here, but I can't seem to form more words as he gets up and picks up the bag in the corner that I hadn't even noticed.

I can understand that he's overwhelmed, I just wish that he'd let me be the one to help him through it rather than pushing me away.

Sam

I'm cleaning the kitchen and making Millie some breakfast when I hear a knock on the door.

I peer through the peep-hole to see Alex looking straight at me. I open the door, feeling wrong-footed after Ruby phoned me last night.

"Alex, I'm sorry about yesterday. I jumped to conclusions and I was worried. What happened?" I ask, standing aside so he can walk past me into the kitchen.

"The nurse said I'd suffered some kind of panic attack brought on by shock. Kate's sister was at my door, she said Kate had died in the morning and she was upset, saying it was my fault . . . I was shaken and found an old bottle. I was trying to pour it away but I just passed out "I tail off, thinking this is enough of an explanation without adding in my journey to Luke's house and the rest of the news I'd had in the last few days.

"God, that must have been awful . . . I just found you and assumed the worst. I'm so sorry" I place a hand on his arm and I see him flinch but he lets it stay there.

"I can see why you did after how you've seen me act in the past, Sam. I just wish you'd waited to hear me out before you went charging off to Ruby" He leans back on the counter as I push two rounds of bread into the toaster that have been waiting there, neglected, since I opened the door.

"I know; I should have trusted you. Is there anything I can do to make things better?" I ask, wanting to put things right.

"Well, Mae's due home tomorrow but Ruby's mum is staying for a few days to help them settle back in and I think I should give Ruby some time with her mum while we work things out. Would you mind if I stayed on the sofa for a night or two?" He asks, those big blue eyes wide and innocent.

"Of course, but don't you want to be there when Mae comes home?" I reply, not wanting to pry any more than I have, so I turn away to butter Millie's toast.

"I'll go and see her, but I'm not sure Ruby and I are in the best place to move forward yet" He sighs, munching on a spare piece of toast that I place in front of him.

"Things will work themselves out Alex, but you can't hide from them" I say, picking up a plate and leaving him to digest my words as I wander upstairs.

Alex

I almost jump out of my skin as I hear my phone beep to signal a text message.

I bend down to retrieve it from my backpack and realise that I must have been lost in my thoughts for a while – The film that I was watching on Millie's TV has been replaced with some kind of chat show. I unlock my phone and see that I have two messages. The most recent is from Nick at work, asking him to ring to update him on any news. There's one from an hour ago from Ruby and I scan it quickly for news.

Hi, we're safely back. Mae misses her daddy, we'd both like you to come home. I love you xx

Something in the tone of the text, as well as what Sam said to me earlier, makes me suddenly ache to see my family. I leave my things at Millie's – I know I still need some time - and take the train back to Southampton to visit my girls.

I find myself knocking on my own front door as I turn the key, only to find Joy sitting on my sofa watching daytime TV. She narrows her eyes at me, so discreetly that I may have imagined it. She turns the volume down while putting a finger to her lips.

"Ruby and Mae are sleeping. Did you come to talk to her?" She asks, motioning for me to join her on the sofa.

"I came to see Mae and to make sure they're settling back in OK" I reply, suddenly uncomfortable in my own skin as well as my own home.

"Do you not think that might be confusing for both of them? Coming to see them but staying somewhere else?" I hear contempt in Joy's voice, which feels like goose bumps on my skin.

"I know how it must seem Joy, but I do love them both. That hasn't changed, but I just need some time to sort the last week out in my head" I look up at her, knowing that this must sound awful, but it's the truth.

"Alex, you know I've always liked you. I was so happy when you and Ruby got together and decided to start a family, because I knew that you had loved her for a long time" She locks eyes with me as she pauses, and I take a deep breath, scared of what she's about to say,

"I was there the morning after Mae must have been conceived. Ruby was scared, so much so that she wouldn't talk even to me properly about what she thought might have happened. I knew that something was wrong, but I told her to put it behind her and to focus on her life with you. I've now got to forgive myself for encouraging her to ignore . . . rape "She whispers the word, covering her mouth as if to trap it inside. She gulps back a few silent sobs before pulling herself back together.

"I can only do that if you help her too. I know that you love her, and I can't understand how you would rather abandon her than trust her after all this time. You know deep down that she wouldn't go back to Luke, but the fact that you've pushed her away when she's found out that she was assaulted and needs your support. . " She sighs and shifts in the seat, and I see a lone tear snaking its way down her cheek.

"Alex, I know that this last week has been a shock to you. It's been a shock to all of us, Ruby included, and I know that you two have a lot to work out. All I ask is that you think about how much time and love you've both put into this relationship. Mae is the product of a love that I saw a long time before the rest of you did, but that love came through her upbringing. I've seen you with her so many times, and no one can say that you don't adore her. Are you really willing to give that up, just because you don't want to face the reality of what happened? You can't seriously believe that Ruby would go back to Luke after he hit her? Have some faith in her Alex, and don't wait too long to clear your head. Ruby and Mae are going to need you, if you're up to being a dad again" She stops, and I look up from my thoughts to see her stood up, opening my front door and gesturing that I should leave.

"I'll tell Ruby that you came round and that you'll be in touch" She says with a slight smile, closing the door before I have the chance to reply.

Sam

I can hear Alex moving about downstairs, and wonder whether I'm the right person to help him through his current situation.

I've always liked Alex, even when I didn't agree with his life choices. In the months before he and Ruby got together, I struggled to be his friend and his boss, but he somehow managed to build himself into someone that I'm proud of.

Neither of us has been into the Night Light since the accident: Alex has been on compassionate leave while Mae's been in recovery, while I don't actually work there anymore. I take a deep breath, wondering what the hell I'm meant to do with myself. I obviously won't be going anywhere near Bristol now that my ex-boyfriend has proven himself to be a lying, cheating... I suddenly remember my conversation with Millie and realise that I haven't mentioned Ben to the police. Should I just forget it all, knowing I never want to see him again, or should I make him pay for what he's done to us all? His deceit seems to have been the catalyst for a mass of horrible events that I'm not sure he should get away with.

I pick up my phone from the bedside table, dialling 99 and then letting my thumb hover over the keys before the panic rises in my stomach and I click the red symbol.

I decide that I can only handle one courageous act for now. I roll out of bed, putting my phone in the pocket of my dressing gown as a reminder of what I should do, and pad downstairs to assure Alex that he isn't the only person who has to figure out how to fit the pieces of his life back together.

Millie

I've been going stir crazy at home – It's been almost a week since I was discharged, but I still feel too sore and tired to be back to work.

I decide that I can probably manage a walk into town, and have an idea that could help Sam. She's been in a terrible state for the last week, reluctant to accept that the man she loved could not only sleep with someone else but also be the evil mind behind a hit and run. I can understand this of course, and I want to give her time to come to terms with things and decide how to move forward.

I knock on the door of the Night Light, finding it odd to look in and not see Sam cleaning tables or planning menus on her laptop. Nick, the Assistant Manager, recognises me with a concerned smile and opens the door. He ushers me inside quickly, and I realise that it's before the 11am opening time.

I look around at the bar that my friend created, having designed the snack bar that had recently been added at the front, and the small platform stage that had been restored against the back wall where it used to be. It's only been two weeks since she sat here with me, excitedly showing me the emails from her head office that agreed to the changes she'd proposed to improve custom. She'd been so sad to resign, the only silver lining being that she'd been accepted for an interview in a similar position at a Bristol bar. The Night Light had always been her baby though, and without her job and her boyfriend she seemed devoid of any kind of purpose or joy. I sit down at the bar, shrugging when Nick asks if there's any news from Alex.

"Mae's back at home recovering, I'm sure he'll be in touch soon" I give him a sad smile, which he returns.

"And Sam?" He ventures, his frown deepening as I meet his gaze.

"Honestly, she's struggling. I've never seen her like this and I'm worried. Have you talked to her since she left?" I ask, leaning forward slightly onto the bar.

"Not really, but I've left a few messages for Alex and asked about her then" Nick looks concerned and I feel suddenly that I've said too much.

I apologise, wishing that I'd talked to Sam before coming in to try and help her. I'm not even sure whether she wants her job back; I just know that she's not herself and that she was really good at this. I tell Nick that I'll be back in soon, but for now I need to see what I can do to help Sam to move past this horrible week.

Sam

I've sat in the lounge in my dressing gown, watching Friends since Alex went upstairs to shower and change.

I hate to admit it, but part of me wants him to stay with us longer than a day or two just so that I won't feel like the only person I know whose life has been shot to pieces.

I have no job, no boyfriend and am currently debating whether to report my ex-boyfriend to the police for something between manslaughter and murder. I haven't let myself think about it, but now that I do, I suddenly see the reason why Alex almost gave himself up to alcoholism. I hear keys in the front door just as I begin to wonder how much wine we have in the fridge. Millie puts her head round the lounge door, instantly brightening my world.

"Hey, how was your walk?" I ask, taking in her red but smiling face.

"It was good, I went to see Nick at the Night Light" She says, walking through to the kitchen and bringing back a bottle and two glasses. I love her in that moment.

"How is he getting on?" I ask, wishing that I still worked there.

"He said that things were good, and all of your changes were still standing. He asked about

Gemma Roman

you though, why don't you go and see him, there might be something available for you?" She replies as I give a sad smile.

"I would Millie, but I don't think I could be less than a manager there. I worked so hard, but Alex took over the reins and I can't ask for my job back now" I sigh, taking a large sip from my glass.

"Perhaps you could talk to Alex? He can't give himself to work just now, you could work something out" She raises her eyebrows as I sigh, not wanting to get my hopes up.

Ruby

I wake up feeling groggy, only to feel tears as I brush my fingers over my face: I've been crying even in my sleep.

I walk through to the lounge, taking a few moments to process that Alex has been replaced with Mum. I love her, but her presence in my home reminds me that something is wrong. She is in the kitchen, entertaining Mae – who is in her high chair munching a banana - as she walks back and forth making scrambled eggs.

"Look who's up!" Mum beams to Mae as she sees me.

Mae squeals with delight, though whether that's at Mum or me I'm not sure. I join them, accepting a cuddle from Mum and a sticky kiss from my daughter. Just knowing that Alex is missing small moments like this makes me sad.

"Eggs and bacon?" She asks, smiling as I nod. She squeezes tomato sauce into the eggs and mixes it in, in the way I've liked since I was old enough to have an opinion.

"Thanks, what time is it?" I ask, knowing that I can't see the clock from here.

"Ten o'clock, have you got deadlines?" Mum sits next to me at the small table, handing me my plate as she does so.

"No new ones. I have a few articles to be

ready by the end of next week, but I contacted the office so I have some leeway" I reply, in between mouthfuls.

I hadn't thought I was hungry, but the contents of my plate are disappearing rapidly. I look up to Mae, who offers me a handful of banana before it slips into her perfectly heart shaped mouth.

"So, how about we all go for a day out somewhere? I think we all need some fun after the last few days" Mum suggests, looking up at me as I finish my plate and get up to pull Mae from the high chair.

I wipe her hands and mouth and give her the cuddle that I missed when she must have first woken up a good three hours ago.

"Would you like to go somewhere Mae? Maybe to the park or the zoo?" I laugh as her face beams.

"Zoo! Zoo!" Is all I hear, as I realise our plans are made.

I take my daughter through to the bedroom to find some clean clothes, wanting to take advantage of having the extra support while my heart aches with my longing to include the one man who doesn't want to be included.

Alex

I open my eyes, hearing the alarm on my phone chirruping at me from the depths of my bag.

I bring myself up to sitting and look across at Millie who is sat on the opposite sofa with a mug of something hot and caffeinated. She smiles at me and reminds me what an amazing friend she is by handing me the mug and walking back through to replace her own coffee.

I take a long sip, knowing that I have to get ready for work, and hopefully at some point in the next few days I can work up the courage to face Ruby – and maybe her mother – to forge a way forward for our family.

I pick up my bag and almost run into Sam on my way to the bathroom. I mutter a quick apology, knowing I need to be at work within the hour to make up for having taken a lot of time off without so much as a phone call to Nick. I feel guilty that it was Millie who informed me that Nick was worried and short staffed, so I finally rang him last night only for him to offer me the lunch shift today in which to prove I was still up to the task of managing the snack bar. I need this job if I'm going to sort things out with Ruby and be able to support the three of us, so it all hinges on today.

I get showered and dressed, not feeling nervous about the job that I've come to know and love, but about the family that I know I need to suddenly prove myself to.

Millie

I made the decision to go back into work for a half day, knowing that I was still in need of rest but also that I've never been the kind of person who can sit around the house for longer than a few days without starting to lose my mind.

I spend a few hours planning the week ahead, feeling productive and keen to arrange some workshops. As lunch time draws near, I feel like I should visit Alex and see how his first day back is going.

I can imagine that he'll be struggling to focus on work when he's not seen Mae since she was discharged, but I also need to do something to help Sam to put her life back together. I open the door, glad to see the bar crowded with customers. Nick and Alex both seem rushed off their feet, but as they work their way through the queues I see that my favourite bar stool is free.

"Hey, are you hungry?" Alex catches my eye and smiles as he finishes serving the customer in front of me.

"Yes, I'm starving! Have you got any sandwiches left?" I peek round to the snack shelves.

"We have one of your favourites left, the chicken and pesto Panini?" He laughs as my face lights up. I hand him the payment, most of which he puts back in my palm. I begin to argue but he cuts me off.

"You've had me staying on your sofa for most of the week, so you're more than welcome to the staff discount" He says with a wink, leaving me to nibble my lunch as he returns to the customers that have formed another queue while we were talking.

The panini is lovely, and is one of the reasons that I'd come to love having the Night Light just a short walk away from my shop. It's made me feel guilty, though, for being here while Sam isn't at work, but I've seen how busy it's been and how much they could surely still use Sam to keep things running smoothly. Alex wipes down the counters once the rush has died down, then returns to see that I've finished my lunch.

"Can I get you anything else?" He asks, but I pat my stomach and blow my cheeks.

"No thanks, they're so nice but so filling" I giggle, passing him my plate.

"I can't believe how busy it is!" I continue, looking round to see that a number of tables still have people relaxing and munching.

"I know, the students are back, but we've lost a few of the staff too. They were studying away and so now we're short staffed but it's hard to find staff who are willing to work a lunch shift as well as a night shift in a bar" He smiles, and I see how much he's actually enjoying his job. He always had the potential as management – I remember Sam saying so – but Mae made him realise that he needed to apply himself and now he's really enjoying the challenge.

"Do you need someone full time? I know Sam would be interested to come back" I venture, wondering what his reaction will be.

"I know she would, and I was just talking to Nick about that actually. He's getting married in a few months and they want to travel on their honeymoon. I suggested that he talk to Sam so at least she'd have the chance of temporary management work. Do you think she'd be interested?" He asks, smiling.

"She loved working here, and just seeing her ideas being successful make me sad that she's not here to see it herself. I don't think she feels as if she can ask to come back, but if she knew that you needed help, she'd jump at the chance. I can talk to her if you like?" I suggest, and he nods. I look at my phone and realise that I should get back home and see how she is.

I wave goodbye to Alex and Nick, walking up the hill with a smile as I potentially have news that could pull Sam back from the void of depression that is threatening to swallow her.

Ruby

I've spent the last hour sat in front of my laptop, ignoring the screen and scrolling through my phone instead.

Mum has taken Mae to the park, and I had promised to go into work over the next few days to talk to my boss and work out the best way to manage articles while sorting things out at home. I'd also promised to email through the remaining articles tonight, most of which are complete but I have a few left to edit and finish off.

That's what today is for: Tying up any loose ends and emailing my boss to confirm tomorrow and send through my work. I've been proof reading an article but my mind keeps wondering to Alex and so I'd zoned out a few minutes ago and found myself reading through old texts and hovering over the 'call' button beside his number.

He would probably be at work now, so it would be safe to ring and leave a message to see how he is or just show him that I miss him. He asked for space, and I agreed to give him that, so I should let him come to me when he's ready. I think of Mae, and the eyes that I'd always thought had come from Alex. I remember talking to Mum that morning in Brighton, feeling that something was wrong, but part of me obviously didn't want to delve deeper. Maybe I should have made myself deal with things then, but I never saw this coming, and now I have no idea how to make things right. I know that I would never have had sex with Luke while Alex was waiting at home for me, but can I blame Alex for believing that over the idea of Luke once again showing the violent temper that frightened me into leaving him in the first place?

I can't put into words how scary it is to discover that during a drunken night out, I was knocked out and... I can't even say the word.

Raped.

I'm not sure whether it's worse to remember something like that, or to never feel the closure that comes from the clarity of knowing. I suppose for now I have no choice, I just have to wait in the hope that Alex will love me enough to trust that I would never betray him like that.

Sam

I wish I could say that I've had a productive day, but I just can't seem to get out of my pyjamas.

Over the last week, my whole life has collapsed on itself, and I have no idea how to sort it out. I've spent my nights – and some of the days – sleeping. I know I need to do something soon, but I just can't motivate myself to move.

I hear keys in the front door, and am confronted with Millie's beaming face before I can turn the channel over from Jeremy Kyle. I'd been watching Diagnosis Murder, so must have been lost in my thoughts for a while if I hadn't noticed the programme change.

"Hey, how was your day?" She asks, and I feel my eyes fill with tears before I can form a reply.

Millie drops her bags and envelops me in a huge hug before my tears find their way down my cheek.

"My day was as shit as my last week has been. Millie, what am I going to do?" I ask, in between sobs. My best friend holds me, letting me cry without words. We've been through a lot of ups and downs, but I'm not sure that I've faced a time more uncertain or scary than this.

"I might be able to answer that" She says, relaying her conversation with Alex earlier today.

"Do you think Nick would be willing to have me back, won't he be back after a few weeks?" I ask, not wanting to get my hopes up.

"I don't know, Alex said that Nick wanted to travel for a few months at least after getting married so he'll at least need temporary cover. What do you think?" She smiles, and I realise after a moment that I'm smiling too.

There's a knock at the door, and I feel my heart rate quicken at the thought that Alex has come round to offer me some version of my job back.

"Hey, how was your day?" I ask Alex as his head appears in the doorway.

"Hi, it was good to be back but it's so busy. Your lunch idea has completely taken off!" He laughs, falling onto the opposite sofa with a sigh.

"Wow, sounds good. I wish I could have seen it through" I sigh myself, but with regret.

"Did Millie tell you about Nick's plans? I think there could be room for you to come back" He looks at me, smiling.

"She mentioned it, but won't he be coming back?" I ask.

"Maybe, but he's excited about travelling so I wouldn't be surprised if they were away for a while. Surely it's worth talking to him?" He suggests, his smile widening as his eyes lock with mine.

I relax back into the sofa as Millie brings mugs of steaming coffee through to us. I reach for the biscuits that I left on the table after lunch, and settle in to hear about their day now that I might once again have job prospects.

Alex

I've been covering the counter for about half an hour on my own and I'm shattered.

I know that this is part of Nick's training – to see if I can handle all aspects of running the bar – and it's fun, but I hope they'll be out of the office soon. Sam has come in today to talk with him about a possible return, so I'm anxious to see what will happen when they come out.

The queue finally comes to an end and I start to clean the counter. There are still a few people sat at tables, so I check my phone for the time. It reads 14:32 but my heart races at the sight of a message from Ruby.

Alex, I know I said I'd give you space but I miss you. I just want to know you're OK and that we can move forward somehow. We love you, take care xx

I find myself feeling breathless and ask Nicole – our one remaining part timer – to cover the counter while I go into the staff room to gather myself.

There has never been any question that I love Ruby, or that I want to be Mae's father. The question to me has been whether I can let myself believe that my own shortcomings were the reason that we've arrived in this unsure, horrible place. I'm not sure I can forgive myself if just when

Ruby needed me, I had given in to my weakness for numbness. I remember being so disappointed when she'd chosen to go out with Amy that night, and rather than stepping up and waiting for her to come home, I'd lost myself in vodka and oblivion rather than face my own company. Either way, that's no reason to let my family continue alone without me. I want so much to reassure Ruby and to let her know that it's myself I'm angry with, not her. I'm just so afraid that doing that would result in her realising that I was never the man she thought I was.

Ruby

So, I'm not ashamed to admit that I gave in and text him.

If I had spoken to Sam or Millie, they probably would have told me to wait and let him come to me, but I couldn't let my life continue in limbo if there was something I could do to resolve this.

I don't know if it will do any good: I sent the message over an hour ago and there has still been no reply, but I have faith that reminding him of us might jolt Alex out of this little bubble he's chosen to retreat into. I can only wait in the hope that he hasn't left us completely, but there's no way to know until he decides to reply or come and finally see his daughter. Regardless of blood, Mae will always be his daughter, but it's all up to him as to whether she grows up knowing that, or whether we have to work our way through this with just the two of us. It would break my heart to keep our family going without Alex – the man who pushed me to believe that we should start the family to begin with – but maybe I'll have no choice.

Time will tell whether we can survive with or without him, and that scares me more than I want to admit.

Sam

I'm happy to say that today I feel as if I've turned a corner.

Thanks to Millie and Alex, I arranged a meeting with Nick to discuss a way forward and to find out if there's still a place for me at the bar that I always loved.

Nick was very understanding, perhaps due to the fact that I was close to tears when I gave my notice in a month or so ago. I never wanted to leave, but love will do foolish things to you. So, I sat with Nick for half an hour, explaining my pathetic situation and my willingness to return to this job in whatever capacity I could. It would have been tough to come back and not be in charge, but with his wedding on the horizon, he's keen to take a back seat and so has offered me a temporary contract as Assistant Manager for three months. He seemed keen to spend some time travelling with his new wife, but assured me that even if he came back to the area soon, there were many other bars opening that would be interested in someone with my 'vision'.

I walk out of the office with a smile on my face, and sit down with Alex to discuss plans for the next few months. He laughs at my constant smile, welcoming me back and telling me how happy he is that I'll be working with him again. It will be strange to work under Alex, but I know that we'll make a good team and I'm lucky to have this chance when I really need something to hold onto.

Alex

I can't figure out a decent reply for Ruby's text, but I can't deny that I've been unable to think of much else since I read it.

I try to distract myself by chatting to Sam about her imminent return, which is fun but can't take my mind away from my family. Should I go and see her, talk things through and forge a way forward? I know I should admit that it's not her that I blame for any of this, but I'm not sure I can say the words out loud again.

She deserves to know that she's not the reason I left, but can I admit that I might not be the person she needs? I'm so scared that she'll work it out for herself in the meantime, which makes me think I should probably go and talk to her before things become more estranged than they already are.

I get on the train after work and once again find myself knocking on my own front door: It feels odd, but somehow I don't feel right barging in when Joy is likely to be there. The door opens to reveal Ruby, looking dishevelled and beautiful in jeans and the Oasis t shirt that she was wearing the first time she ever kissed me. The memory makes me happy and sad all at the same time, wondering how likely it will be that we can get back to that place.

"Come in" She says, not fully smiling but still

letting me in. I hope this is a good sign and follow her into the lounge.

"How are you both doing?" I ask, aware how weird it is to be asking that of my own family.

"As good as can be expected I suppose" She replies, sitting down with a sigh, acknowledging silently that I don't need or want a host in my own flat.

"Ruby, we need to talk, I know that. I'm not really sure what to say to make things better or to make you forgive me for leaving but I can't go on like this. I can't let you and Mae get used to life without me, but I need to know that you want me to come back and that you don't hate me for taking some time out" I take a deep breath, glad to have said all that but hoping that Ruby's reply won't be too harsh or angry.

"Alex, I can't pretend you didn't hurt me. I've never lied to you, but you made it clear that you would doubt that almost as a reflex. I know it's a difficult situation, but I needed your support and you denied me that. I don't know what you want from me, but I can't just pretend that it's OK that you would rather doubt me than believe me" Ruby sighs, and I feel it rather than hear it. I feel the heartbreak and the hurt that I've caused her, and I'm suddenly afraid that I've given her too long without me.

"I'm sorry – I'm sorry for all kinds of things. I

should have believed you; I should have stayed and helped you get through this. I should have admitted that I was angry with my own insecurities, not with you. Now I'm scared that I've ruined everything and it might be too late to put it back together" I force myself to stand up, aware that this situation will take more than one conversation to fix.

"Alex?" Ruby's voice breaks, and I look her in the eye for the first time.

"I think we both need some more time, but would you do me a favour? Would you come over again in a few days? I'd like to see you and talk more, and perhaps you could spend some time with Mae" The look on her face melts something inside of me. I nod, allowing myself a small smile.

"Until then" Is all I can say, knowing that my own voice is likely to break at any moment.

I daren't hug her, but instead let myself out of the flat and walk downstairs in a daze. It's only when I'm on the pavement outside that I allow myself a few moments to think through the last ten minutes. I collapse on a step and find myself forcing deep ragged breaths, trying to keep the inevitable tears at bay.

Millie

I hear Sam's keys in the door and wait for her to walk into the lounge.

I haven't heard from her all day, but Alex rang to tell me the good news so I could buy a bottle of champagne on my way home from work. I'm so happy that Sam was able to get some semblance of a job back, and as she walks through to greet me, the beam on her face assures me that she shares my relief.

"So, you had a good day?" I ask, handing her a glass as I pick up the bottle.

"I have a temporary contract for Nick's job, which is risky, but who knows how much he'll enjoy travelling with Connie?" She replies, accepting the glass and wincing slightly as I manage to pop the cork. The familiar knock on the door sounds as we pour the fizzy liquid across two glasses. This time, we lock eyes with a sad expression, having hoped that Alex and Ruby would have worked things out by now. Sam's face is less surprised, and I wonder if she talked to Alex at work as she backs into the hallway

Sam opens the door quietly, and I move towards the doorway as I hear unfamiliar voices. She ushers me into the kitchen as I see flashes of police badges and give her a confused look. She smiles but her eyes give away an underlying fear.

We show the two officers into the lounge as Sam takes another sip of champagne – perhaps for courage – and we sit down to discuss the night that changed everything.

Alex

I sit on the train in a state of confusion, to the point where I almost miss my stop.

It's weird to be thinking of it as my stop, when it's the opposite journey that I take to go home but such is our current situation. I arrive at Millie's door and raise my hand to knock as I see the police car parked outside. Sam opens the door looking like an animal caught in headlights, and I meet her eyes with a look that I hope conveys worried confusion. She takes my hand and leads me into the lounge, where my bag still lies beside the sofa. Sat on the sofa are two officers, with kind but serious faces as they look up to see the new arrival.

"This is Alex, Mae's father" Sam says by way of introduction, and I'm sure she's the only one that can sense me flinch at the lie she just told.

"What's going on?" I ask, not knowing what else to say as I sit down next to Millie.

"Alex, Sam said that you found out about Kate's death after the crash. I'm sorry" Millie says gently, putting her own hand over mine on the seat. I sigh, almost as reflex, but feel less sadness than anger.

"That's a shame for her family, but wasn't she the reason for the crash?" I surprise myself at the lack of emotion for someone I used to love, but all

I can think of is Mae.

"Actually some new evidence has come to light. We should go, but I'm sure your friends can fill you in on the details. Keep us informed of anything that might be of interest" The taller officer says as they walk back through the door, shaking my hand as they pass.

"What the hell was that about?" I look to Sam for some form of explanation.

"There's something you need to know about the accident, Alex. You will never know how guilty I feel for this but I can't keep it from you anymore" She says, and I see her eyes fill up with tears as she recounts that night. It's bizarre to think that it was only a week ago, when all of our lives have changed so much since then.

I can't quite grasp the details of what Sam is saying, but I'm trying to because I know that it's the reason that my life is falling apart. I hear Ben's name – a man that I actually considered a friend until I heard about what had happened in Bristol – and anger fills my veins like a drug on behalf of Sam. My friend who has seen me through some of the worst times in my life, and she is recounting something so traumatic that I can see her trembling as she talks.

Part of me seems to be taking in the details, and even though I can't deny I'm starting to freak out at the truth, I can see that Sam is freaking out more and needs my support.

It occurs to me that the last thing I said to Kate was that I blamed her for the crash, when the likelihood was that she was just as much a victim as Mae. It also occurs to me that while I have been in my own self – involved bubble, Sam has been not only tied up in confusion and pain over her own life, but also been feeling guilty over knowing the real reason for the crash and been unable to tell me. That's all I see as I look into her eyes, guilt and fear. Fear that she will lose my friendship after sharing nothing but honesty on a day when she should be celebrating getting part of her life back. I'm her boss after being her employee, and I feel the sudden need to reassure her.

"Sam, it's not your fault" I say, looking deep into her eyes as I speak, and holding her hand.

She blinks in surprise, obviously expecting me to shout or walk out. As she blinks, her face collapses slightly and she puts her head onto her hands. She sobs freely, as she leans into me and lets out the frustration and pain that we've all been holding inside. I hold her, looking up and locking eyes with Millie as she gives a sad smile, wandering back into the kitchen to fetch the champagne.

Ruby

I sit on the floor, watching Mae sleeping on the sofa.

We went to the park before lunch and she's shattered, almost breathing loudly enough for it to become a little snore. I watch her, wondering how it can really be true that Alex isn't her father. She has his eyes, and she has so many mannerisms of his that I've thought some days she takes more after him than me. Perhaps it's all nurture and the nature element only counts for so much, but I've never looked at her and seen an ounce of Luke.

I resolve that I never will: Whether Alex comes home or not, I won't disrespect him by letting Mae know that her dad is anyone but the man that helped me to raise her and love her for the last few years.

Hearing him admit his real reasons for leaving, I felt something inside of me shift. I had thought that he was doubtful of me, of how much I love him. Knowing that all he doubts is himself fills me with nothing but fear and regret. Regret that we seem to have fallen so far apart from each other that neither of us understood the other, and fear that this could lead Alex back on the self-destructive path I found him on.

Would he really do that when we have Mae to consider? His love for us both has shone through on his last few visits, despite our discussions. He's been a heartbroken shell of the man that I fell in love with, leading my heart to follow him out of the front door each time.

I feel lost in a way that I've never felt before. When things ended with Luke, it hurt me but I knew that we could never be together again: Whatever had happened, I couldn't be with someone who would act violently, whatever the cause.

With Alex, it's the circumstances that are getting in the way, but neither of us can seem to bridge the gap. Our last conversation gave me hope, but I still don't know what will happen, how we can rebuild this.

All I know is that we can't give up. In my heart, I know that I need Alex to be a part of this family, and when I see him I know that he agrees. Whether we can put aside our own issues is another conversation, and who knows how long it will take us to sort this out. Surely, as long as I can look into his eyes and see the emotion that is tearing us both apart, I'll see the love that could pull us back together. We just needed to be apart for a while to realise that it doesn't work, we've loved each other for so long that our lives simply don't make sense without each other to help figure them out. They never have.

At least that's what I let myself hope as I curl

my body around my daughter and smile as she shifts in her sleep, her body instinctively folding itself into the curve of my hip. My heart sinks slightly as I remember waking a few weeks ago as Alex returned home and joined us as we slept. Mae's body fits into mine, but my own skin is longing for the closeness of our missing third. The memory of his hand clinging to my hips and his lips resting against my neck as his breathing slowed, it jumbles in my head until I feel myself begin to weep.

I cry silently, not wanting to wake Mae, but I can't stop the tears as they flow. I force my breathing to slow, and as I do I feel Mae turn over and rest her hand on my waist in the exact position that Alex's was in my memory. It can only be coincidence, but it breaks my heart and I wonder in my confused state whether our daughter's heart might be as affected by the memory of our broken family as Alex and I are.

Ben

My head is a mass of muffled banging, and I turn over in bed to put a pillow over my head.

I'm almost ashamed to admit that I came back to Bristol and sent a text to a certain dance teacher, though even through my muddled hangover I can see that she's not who I brought home last night. This girl is a brunette, though nowhere near as beautiful as the girl who I try not to think about.

My head bangs again, and I wander whether I should get up and have some water to rehydrate. The brunette opens her eyes to look at me and impart some crucial information at this point.

"Get the door, I'm sleeping!" Is all she says, covering herself up with my duvet.

I walk to the front door, meandering across the lounge until I find the dressing gown that I must have left on the floor at some point. The banging has become more incessant now, and I open the door, preparing a look of angry contempt for whoever is invading my morning. I start as I see two police officers standing in front of me, one of whom is holding up a badge.

"Ben Anderson?" He asks, and all I can do is nod.

"Would you mind if we came inside for a few minutes, we have something we need to discuss with you" The other man states, introducing them both whilst walking past me into what must look like a bedsit.

I struggle to think through the fog in my head that has been a constant over the last week. I have had a strong need to feel nothing, but as I'm forced to make eye contact with this man I feel the nausea and panic rise up in my chest as he starts to ask for answers that might lead to a future even darker than the hole I've tried to bury myself in.

Ruby

Part of me would like to spend the rest of my life not knowing, but the other part knows that to move forward I need closure.

That's why I find myself walking up a driveway that I haven't seen for years, strangely familiar as if I'm inside a dream. I knock on the door, waiting for my nerves to settle so I can actually articulate the questions I need answered.

Luke answers the door, and his face pales slightly as he sees my face.

"Ruby" He says, but it sounds more like a question than a statement.

"Hi, I know that Alex has been to see you, and I don't want to cause a scene. I just wondered if you would come for a quick walk with me?" I ask, feeling a weird mixture of unease and pity as he nods and follows me without a word.

We walk along the pavement, and I know I have to begin this conversation, I'm just not sure how to. I take a few deep breaths and force words through my throat before it closes.

"Did Alex tell you about Mae's blood test?" It's both direct and ambiguous as questions go.

He doesn't reply, but as I glance across at him I see his shoulders shake and I stop walking. I realise with dread that he's started crying, and I have no idea whether to comfort him or run. I wait for a few minutes, as he composes himself and finally his eyes meet mine.

"Ruby, I don't know what to say. That night . . . . I was so drunk, and I'd just found out that you and Alex were together after you cheated on me . . . . When I saw you, I just got so angry, and then I kissed you and for a second I thought you were kissing me back. I saw red . . . it was as if I was someone else, like just before we broke up " he looks away and my mind flits back to that horrible night years ago. He sees me flinch, though I say nothing, I just wait for him to continue.

"I thought that it was mutual, I thought maybe you'd closed your eyes and were enjoying it . . . By the time I realised what had happened, we were already . . . I didn't know what to do, I just panicked and . . . Afterwards I ran off, caught the first train home. I never thought that anyone would know, and when Alex showed up at my door . . . He told me about your daughter . . . "He trails off, unsure of how else to dig himself out the hole I'm sure.

Hearing him tell me the truth after all this time makes me wish I hadn't come here. I'd thought that Alex and I couldn't move forward without closure, but now that I know I feel like I might be sick. I start to walk away, needing to get as far from Luke as I can.

"Ruby, please wait!" He follows me, even as I

break into a run, but he catches me up in less than a few feet and grabs my arm.

"Is she my daughter?" His fingers crawl up my sleeve and tangle in my hair, until I have to shake them off.

"No!" I snap, spitting the words out as I yank my arm away.

"You need to listen to me closely . . . No matter what a blood test says, Mae is Alex's daughter and will never be yours. I don't care how drunk you were, or how angry you were with me . . . Maybe as angry as when you hit me, maybe even as angry as I am now. You don't deserve this, but I'm going to do us both a favour. You will never tell anyone else about that night, and if you ever come anywhere near me or my family again, I will take this to the police" I run out of steam, willing the tears to stay behind my eyes as I open my palm to show him the phone I'm holding. I press the screen and his voice – tinny, but clear enough – repeats his pathetic little speech back to him as his eyes close and he sinks onto the nearest brick wall.

"Ruby - "He starts, but I'm already walking away. I don't want to look back and see that face again.

I'm glad that I don't remember that night, and although I feel nauseous at the thought of what happened, all I want is to get back to my family and put this horrible situation behind us.

Sam

sitting

I look up from my desk to see Millie sat at the bar with a smile on her face.

I've got to admit that even though I'd been gone for less than two weeks, the changes have made my return a bit overwhelming. It's so cool to see my plans working out and the lunch rush as busy today as it was on its first day – according to Alex – but it's a lot to contend with.

"Are you here for lunch again?" I ask, reaching for her favourite Panini.

"Yes please, and a coffee. I'm so tired today, and the kids at the workshop were crazy" Millie yawns, but I can see a smile in her eyes.

"What was it today, bracelets?" Alex asks, approaching us after wiping down some tables.

"It started with beaded bracelets but then we moved onto charms after one of the girls saw one I'd made" she laughs, clearly enjoying her day.

"So, are the workshops helping your sales now then?" I ask, taking a pile of papers from Alex.

"They really are - I'm actually in profit over the last month! I'm shattered, but owning your own business will do that!" She giggles, winking at me as I place her lunch on the bar.

"I know! It's not that we own the bar, but just managing things again is a shock to the system after a few weeks off. It's nice working with Alex though, and to have someone that I know to help make the decisions" I smile at Millie as she drinks from the mug.

"We might be a bit late back tonight though. We're still recruiting for extra part timers and need to get interviews set up before we can finalise the live music element" I say, gesturing to the stage area with a handful of CVs.

"Wow, sounds busy! I'll be at home watching a film I think" She replies, brushing crumbs off her fingers.

"Sam, I need to pop out for a moment. Would you mind holding the fort?" Alex appears at my side, his face lit up as he points past Millie to the front door. standing

Ruby is stood outside, hands stuffed in the pockets of her jeans, looking towards Alex with a mixture of happiness and anxiety.

I sat on that brick wall for almost an hour after Ruby walked away from me. The owner of the house shouted from the window in the end to ask me to leave.

I don't know what it is about Ruby, but there's something in her self-deprecating smile, something in the glint of her eyes that seems to draw everyone to love her. It's always been there, but I panicked at the sight of losing her and it led me to a depressing few years living under my parents' roof again and wondering what the hell had happened to my life.

It's almost as if she puts a spell on you, and you have no choice but to want to be near her. I felt the power of that spell for the years we were together, and then I didn't think I'd ever feel that kind of love again.

I've meandered through the streets for a while, but my feet have grown tired so I settle on a lonely wooden bench and lean my head on my fist, my elbow resting uncomfortably on the arm of the bench.

I've tried hard over the last year to not remember the night I raped her. It wasn't something I'd planned on, although looking at our past I don't expect that a jury would believe that.

I had drunk too much, and been so angry that

my ex had become happy with my former best friend. Seeing her outside the pub, I felt like she owed me something after all of that betrayal.

Kissing her again had felt like coming home, and I had let myself get lost in that feeling. We'd seemed to tumble to floor in a rush of passion after a kiss that re-ignited my senses. She closed her eyes, leaning her head back against the cold concrete so I could kiss her neck tenderly and my hands had started to wander to her torso.

I'd felt the overwhelming urge to make love to her, to be close to her again, but suddenly realised that I had no protection. I had not come back here in anticipation of sex, but I was drunk and excited and needed to entice my ex -girlfriend back to me. I wanted to hear her shout my name again – We'd always quite enjoyed experimenting with outdoor locations, but outside a pub hadn't been a turn on before.

I lifted her skirt and pulled aside her black, lacy underwear – which turned me on even more – and had entered her with a single movement. As I began to move into a rhythm, I sensed that Ruby wasn't moving with me and so had re-focused on her face. I saw that her eyes were closed and so touched her face so she'd look at me.

She didn't wake up.

I panicked, the intensity of the feeling resulting in an abrupt but not unpleasant climax as

I realised what I've just done.

I needed to get out of there, and fast. I pulled her clothes back around her and picked up my things, running back in the general direction of the B and B to grab my belongings and find the next train home.

An old man walks past with his dog and waves a greeting, bringing me back to present day. I run my fists across my eyes, realising with shame that I'd started to cry again.

I'd been so scared when Alex had come to find me, but knowing that all I need to do is stay away so that they won't report me is such a relief. I can live my life again – It's not as if I ever wanted to return to Winchester again anyway, so after all this time it gives me something to be grateful to Ruby and Alex for, and perhaps I can move on.

Ruby

I rang Mum from the train, knowing that I had to go straight to see Alex after enduring the trip to Luke's.

I was trying to think of something profound and impressive to say during the train journey, but as I stand now looking into the window at him, I just want to hold him. I wait outside, wanting to talk with him before I have to make conversation with Sam and Millie. There is so much going on in my head that I'm not sure I can make sense to friends until we've at least started to discuss our relationship in private.

"Hi, how are you?" Alex asks, bending to kiss me on the cheek in an almost awkward gesture.

"I'm fine, can we go somewhere for a few minutes?" I venture, hoping that we can talk away from prying eyes.

"I can't be long; we could go to the cathedral grounds?" He starts to walk, playing with his hands before he follows my lead and puts them in his pockets.

It feels strange to walk with him and not hold his hand, but I don't want to force a physical connection before we work out how to solve the emotional one that we've lost. We walk at a quick pace, both anxious to find our own space away from the busy high street.

The cathedral looks grand and stunning in the autumn sunshine, and we both slow our pace just to look up at it. There are a few groups of students drinking or reading across the grass, but we spot an empty bench on the path and sit down on opposite ends.

"I'm glad you came to see me" He says, looking at me so I can see the hope in those beautiful stormy blue eyes.

"I'm tired of avoiding each other Alex, and I thought that if the two of us could sit down and just talk things through, that we could figure out what comes next and how to get through this" I search his eyes, looking for understanding.

"Ruby, you know I want to get through this. I've spent the last few days sleeping on a sofa and wondering what the hell happened to my life. I was completely dumbstruck at the hospital and I reacted so badly after seeing Luke because I didn't want to face the fact that I might not be good enough for you" He pauses and I frown, waiting for him to continue.

"I never really believed that you would sleep with him, I know you better than that, after what he did to you, especially. What I couldn't handle was that you'd come home in need of support and comfort, and I'd fallen back into the old habit of drinking myself into a state. I left you alone and frightened when you needed me, and that scared me more than the idea of you being unfaithful. How do we move forward after that?" I hear his voice crack and feel a rush of affection for him as he brushes his hand through his hair.

"Alex, it's not your fault" I suddenly can't resist touching him anymore and ruffle my hand through the soft, blonde mess of curls that I've always loved.

I take my phone from my pocket and play Alex the recording that I didn't want to hear again. It's worth it if it can help to mend us and get Alex to finally let go of the anger that he's used to form a noose around his neck. His neck jerks up as he hears Luke's voice, and I see his expression move through a myriad of feelings – surprise, anger, confusion.

"I went to see Luke myself" I say, when I've put my phone away.

"Why would you do that to yourself?" He asks, and I can see that he's struggling to form words through the hatred written on his face.

"I needed to know, Alex. I needed the truth so that I could finally forgive myself and let go of the uncertainty I've carried around" I finally take a breath and look up to see Alex smiling.

"And you don't want Luke to pay for what he did?" Alex looks deep into my eyes, as I realise I'm crying through my own smile.

"Luke has to live with what he's done, and

I've told him that if he ever shows his face again that I'll take this to the police" I say, and the twinkle returns to Alex's eyes.

"So, what happens now?" He asks, his hands playing with a hole in his jeans.

"Now, you go back to work with a smile on your face. Then, when you finish later, you come back home to our family" I reply, a tear returning to my eye as I look up to see his reaction.

"Are you sure?" His eyes are shining, but they look happy for the first time in a while.

"I love you Alex and I think if we can get past this last week, we can pretty much make it through anything. It feels so wrong living in that flat without you, and missing a week with Mae is like missing a year with an adult . . . She's changing so quickly and I want you home so we can see that happen. Maybe in time, you'll even need that ring box again?" I pause to breathe, laughing as I feel how freely the tears are falling. It's nice to feel happy tears after so long.

Alex is quiet for a few moments, though he reaches his fingertips to my cheeks to wipe away my tears. After wiping them away, he reaches out and takes my hand. His fingers intertwine with mine in a way I've always loved. The sudden contact after so much space feels like someone has just switched a light switch back on, and I find myself not wanting to let go.

His phone chirrups in his pocket and he looks down at the display with a sigh.

"I have to get back to work, I'm sorry" He says, replacing the phone into his jacket while his hand still plays with mine on his lap. We stand up, not wanting to break apart after finally working things out.

I turn to walk back, but Alex pulls on my hand and I lean in close to him. I tilt my head up to kiss him, feeling the same rush that I felt on the first night in his flat, the same rush that I denied all those years ago when he first kissed me after too much wine.

I let out a soft moan as we break apart, knowing that he's needed back at the bar. As his hand finds mine on his hip and we walk back through the crowded high street, our fingers mingle again and I know we can start to rebuild the family that we almost lost.

Epilogue:

Ali

I sit on a bench, concealed by the think branch of a large cherry blossom tree.

I watch them talk, holding hands as if they're teenagers planning a second date. It makes me sick, seeing them so happy when my sister is gone. All she'd wanted was Alex; she'd spent seven years of her life trying to build a future with him, only for him to leave her for that boring little brunette.

I keep my eyes on them as they stand up, embrace playfully and then amble back towards the gates that lead out onto the high street. My phone vibrates in my pocket and I see my mother's name on the screen.

"Alison? Are you there?" She asks, sounding worried as usual.

"Hi mum, how are you?" I reply, moving slowly so as not to arouse suspicion.

"We were just wondering when you might be coming home? Your sister's funeral will be next week, once we can get the... body back here." I hear a slight sob as she tries to keep her composure, knowing that my dad will be holding her hand.

"I'll be back in a few days, and I can help you

to arrange any extra bits for the service. I think I might come back here in a few weeks though; there are a few things I want to talk to Alex about. A few things he still has of hers" I say gently, knowing my parents won't be pleased.

I say goodbye, promising to ring them later, knowing that they need my support. But so did Kate.

She came back here for closure, and she lost her life, and somehow all of that revolved around Alex and Ruby and their precious little child.

I owe it to her to get the closure she deserved, and I'll make sure I do.

Acknowledgements / Note from the Author

As this was my first novel, many people helped me along the way – Jan Pugh (or mum, as I often call her) for reading the very first draft and supporting my long-standing dream to become an author since I was perhaps old enough to hold a pen. Thanks to Beth Wooldridge, Sarah Hughes, Sarah Anwar, Jill Lloyd, Sian Snape and Rebekah Hill for your suggestions, as well as your support and for not laughing at my dreamy ambition! Thanks especially to Rebekah Hill and Jacob Prytherch for the beautiful cover art, and to Jacob Prytherch and Matty Millard for your wise advice, expertise and patience.

To anyone else reading this: Thank you for taking a chance on a new author - If you've enjoyed it, please be so kind as to rate and review it at amazon.com.

Printed in Great Britain
by Amazon